Lethal Assumed

Lost Tome Found

JEFFREY UNDERWOOD

iUniverse, Inc.
Bloomington

Lethal Assumed
Lost Tome Found

iUniverse books may be ordered through booksellers or by contacting:

iUniverse
1663 Liberty Drive
Bloomington, IN 47403
www.iuniverse.com
1-800-Authors (1-800-288-4677)

ISBN: 978-1-4759-0004-0 (sc)
ISBN: 978-1-4759-0005-7 (ebk)

Printed in the United States of America

iUniverse rev. date: 03/21/2012

Not for Eighteen and Under

Contents

Introduction

Forbidden Tome; Hansel and Gretel's True Tale left many questions unanswered. What becomes of the surviving characters? What is the Tome? Who writes the Tome? What does its discovery prove to the world at large? What mysterious being is at work sorting through the age old conundrum of what reigns supreme, love or violence?

Lethal Assumed; Lost Tome Found reveals not only resolution to much that is raised in the first tale but itself does not disentangle all. Such as this query: what is it that is generally assumed about creatures beyond human comprehension? Humans often allow their fear of the unknown to guide their presumptions. Fear taints and darkens expectations. Considerations incline toward the suspicious, the sinister, and the violent and malicious then. But wait! What if it is an instinct that creates greater rather than lesser difficulties for people? Might creatures beyond human ken have as deep set values as any person is capable of? Is it arrogance to believe that good predominates amongst mortals only? Find out here.

This is a story that synthesizes the big and the small in the Forbidden Tome. The time in Lethal Assumed has now become present day Seattle, the Emerald City by the sea. A beautiful, young ballerina develops uncertainties about her lover, Marius. In her search for the truth of his fidelity to her, she journeys fearfully and far. There is much mystery that propels her forward. She has allies who, in moments of grave doubt about the safety of her quest, assist in her discovery of the lost tome. The accident of its finding reveals so much.

Clearly, Amanda, the brave and wantonly beautiful ballerina is rarely prepared for the unraveling; the truth of her Marius. And what of Marius's reaction? Does he respond sweetly to her suspicions or no? He must protect himself; aggressively one would assume. Does he choose himself, Amanda or a blend unforeseen in the beginning?

And what of those left suspended in the first tale? What is their fate? How real are Hansel and Gretel? What of their fortune? Are they just figments of the Brothers Grimm imaginations or are they more?

The intricacies are many, the fears are vast and the echoes of significance repeat without end. Let the mind relax as this second tale is told. Let that mind drift and be pulled. Not a reader of Lethal Assumed will regret that decision.

Acknowledgments

As Always to My Muse And Ever Supportive Wonder
Penny Woodward

Also Thank You For Your Character Inspiration

Rose Smith
Amanda Nations
My Marvel Kate
Marius Petipa
The Beautiful City of Seattle
Sweet Judith

Finally, my heartfelt appreciation to all of those who make
authoring a book accessible
And possible.

Chapter 1

BODY TUNED

Her delicately sinuous leg stretched fully up to the barre. Second nature to her, chest was flattened to leg, ankle and knee supported by the elongated oak rail; she held that position for a count of thirty. In her novice days, Amanda's calf muscles-her gastrocnemii to be specific—quivered almost painfully at completion of this most basic of warm-up poses. Very gracefully and with careful composure in order to not strain herself, Amanda switched to the identical pose with her other leg.

She had just hurried inside. Then she doffed her hooded windbreaker, which protected her from the distraught wind and whipsawed Seattle rain storming in the dark outside, and flung it into a quick studio corner. He was present and she did not desire erring on her pre rehearsal exercises any more than she had already erred with her unfortunate tardiness. Though he leaned casually backwards in a slightly tipped and roughed up director's chair with hands clasped at neck base, his focused glance bestowed upon Amanda brooked no further transgressions on her part. So, though her initial routine came automatically, she was very careful to exert caution and intelligence as she rolled totally through her drills.

1

Feeling a bit of insouciance, she smiled casually, intersecting his glance perfectly. She occasionally enjoyed plucking him from his stern rigor and rigid expectations.

She loved Marius well though. Wise or no, they had plied their attraction together to a level that carried far beyond the professional. She was young yet and so had found that her impulses overcame her better judgment. Now that they were irrevocably intertwined, she prayed that he and she would maintain a consummate integrity in regards to all aspects of their company's performance of the beloved Giselle.

Amanda was proud to have won Marius over and had been chosen to play the heroine.

Amanda was also so enthralled with her character Giselle that she had even contemplated changing her first name to the very same as the wondrous female in this ballet. The heart of Giselle was enormous to Amanda despite its fundamental fragility.

The old Germanic tale that supported the ballets structure mesmerized Amanda. She was unable to imagine a soul braver, more romantic than or as forgiving as her storied young twin, Giselle. Amanda's largest muscle, her brain, was pouring over the plot all the while that her other muscles were being softly prepared for a bout of soon to be tense exertion.

Grape harvest in the Rhineland was a sweeping and hugely anticipated event. Frail, lovely Giselle was held back from joining the joyous laboring throngs methodically separating the finest clusters from the rest and then transporting them in the sturdy woven baskets to be destemmed and crushed underfoot.

Amanda fantasized the free running juices exploding from beneath the stomping soles. She discerned the pleasure that Giselle must have experienced as wine barrels were filled and the celebrations began.

Sadly, the spirited Giselle was closely managed by her mother; a mother who agonized over her daughter's infirmities and congenitally weakened heart.

As Giselle ran from the cottage with her mother, Berthe, upon her heels, she would become mindful and would stop abruptly, only to watch the grape picking hoard select the best and finest of clusters.

Amanda, sensitive being that she was, felt Giselle's pain at those physical limitations imposed upon her. Amanda had no such physical limitations but that did not interfere with her empathetic ability to place herself in another's skin.

En pointe now, toe tips blocked and barely contacting the floor, Amanda preened and spun for her mentor though this was not her customary progression through her limbering maneuvers. She adored exhibiting her lush skills and lithe beauty for Marius to absorb.

Now back to her further plies and whimsical concoctions of Giselle and her cherished adventures.

She immediately fixated on her image of Duke Albrect, a nobleman of princely look but, unfortunately, less than princely behavior. Damn him and his loutish ways, Amanda ruminated; typically he was a self-centered and voraciously insensitive male. She pictured him though as robust, magnificently handsome and devastatingly charming either as a lord or as a peasant; lord he was, peasant he only pretended.

His particulars began simply enough. He craved to sew some wild oats before he became married to Bathilde, daughter of the neighboring Prince of Courland. He loved and cherished his Bathilde yet cherished his freedom equally. Well aware of that shrinking liberty, he felt the need to spread his seed one last time. And he did not hesitate to put his plan into play regardless of risk.

As she felt her body nearly warmed and tuned, Amanda deliberated further on how Giselle innocently tumbled into the Duke's connivances. He intended to quickly woo a gorgeous naïve peasant girl as a peasant himself, Loys.

Amanda deemed his actions to be absolutely pathetic. She understood that Giselle would become his dupe and fall hopelessly in love with this master of machinations and deceit. And, as well, his bride to be, Bathilde, deserved a partner who was true and honest. Amanda, as a romantic to her depths, was angered at males who consciously victimized females emotionally, stole their hearts and love, and then cruelly departed once their uncaring needs were satisfied. It had happened to her once already in her fledgling life.

As she finished off the last of a front tendu, she whipped a harsh sudden stare in the direction of Marius. He noticed and jerked up from his chair in a concerned approach towards Amanda. She needed a few reassuring words from him and was pleased that she was about to receive comfort from him.

"Amanda, you startled me. I felt a distinct shadow in your glimpse of me just now."

He touched her waist with one large long-fingered hand at each side and guided her body as if instructing her. As she peered down at his hands, he whispered in her ear, "I love you my sweet and most gorgeous Amanda. That is sincere and genuine, never false. Thank you for returning that to me."

Amanda was pacified. His and her instincts supported one another automatically.

Chapter 2
HIS SORROW

He surveyed all who entered the studio and acknowledged their arrival without a word exchanged. And, yes, it annoyed him that his Giselle was not present and at the barre at the very top of the hour. Being severely constrained by the twenty four hour clock himself created an attention in him toward others habits of promptness as well. And, of course, this was his troupe and they needed to mind a rigorous discipline for the sake of the gem which they would stage play soon enough.

Ah, but Amanda was rarely late and so he was calm when the doors exploded open and she nearly lunged for the barre in order to pin herself to her stretches. Her breathless dash to the mirrored wall and handhold included a desperate and haphazard toss of her rain slicked hoodie to the floor.

Upon observing this entrance, he went beyond calm to being helplessly and hopelessly amused at her wonderful innocence and want to be at her natural best at all times. So it was delicious also when her humanity was as tenderly revealed as it was now. He rigorously kept his smile beneath a placid surface but the light in his eyes would not be held at bay and gave him away to anyone paying close attention; no one was, though, because they all attended to their lovingly paced and totally scripted loosening movements.

His field of vision locked in upon her. Her hair, in free fall, was this glorious silken river of pale blonde tresses naturally streaked with intermittent golden threads that draped past her bottom. And, as if that was not luscious enough by itself, a widow's peak formed at the perfect top center of her forehead. She hardly noticed though as she whipped her mane to and fro without self-consciousness or thought. When she flipped her hair over her shoulders, as she often did, it was because she was impatient with its interference; never to show off or flirt. Marius knew, laughingly, that one would be able to find his way through the darkest environments illumined only by her bright locks.

But of course, this was not her singular physical gift. She had the prototypical ballerina's gorgeous face with a difference. This difference set her apart immediately and vividly from all of her competing peers. No, it was not the flawlessly set piercing sapphire eyes that dazzled with a fine fluttering, fascinatingly long twin shelf of lashes. Nor was it her delicately honed and barely noticed, though regal in all aspects, high tipped nose; and, if not exactly regal, it was an absurdly sweet characteristic. Nor was it the high arched cheekbones that gave Amanda the appearance of Aphrodite created especially for feminine ideals of the modern American era. And it was not her full yet not overly plump, gracefully elongated, delicately curved lips.

Marius lingered upon what set her visage apart. There was this inner shine, a rich luminosity that manifested itself upon her brow, at upturned lips, rosy hued small cheeks, sparkling sheen of iris and sclera glowing. It was as if the light of her soul gleamed transparently off of her countenance. And, obviously, what a captivating soul it was.

Honestly, he loved her without reserve. He had not experienced this mixed pleasure and bane for many a year.

He thought back to those many years ago.

It was his sorrow that he had never convinced this other woman that he had truly loved her. She had left him, fled was the more apt description, in utter haste and disgust.

Their last mutually received encounter was riven with outsize emotion and behavior. He recalled even the nuances of that rapturous enfolding and then disastrous recoil into realms of shock, disbelief and then her dynamic, determined departure from his embrace.

For him, those events had been hell on earth. Her faith in his sentiment toward her had dissolved instantly. She gave him no leave, no moment for him to plead for their union; she merely stood above him, glared down upon him, then departed in a rush.

The eve had begun in pure, spontaneous passion. He and she had danced and sung brilliantly through an ancient ballet. The gathered audience had clapped adoringly and repeatedly. He and she had removed their masks, bowed humbly any number of times. Not named that then, it was their response to multiple curtain calls.

This object of his desire and love, so like Amanda in spirit, moderately dissimilar in appearance, was proudly sharing her after performance bliss with him; her mentor, stage partner, lover. It was then that the unraveling began.

He and she were enlivened by one another's touch. He was drawing upon one of her firm and aroused jet black nipples. Her dancer's tights were all that remained upon her body. He had already ripped her top apart so that he had complete access to her torso. He was clothed still but hungered, ached, for her large mounded chest. And she shared her breasts with him urgently. She gripped his hair with one hand and crushed his head deeper into her cleavage.

Then she removed her tights from those lean, strong, ebony legs of hers.

The room was backlit and warm from a blazing hearth fire. He remembered that aspect so well. He cherished those fires and it served to symbolize their united heat. The fire enlarged and crackled more. She and he remained fused to one another. He felt her at her parted legs; her wet core. He spread her nether lips and they were slick, sticky and tenderly hot. He felt her pulse that was so hard upon her as he momentarily rubbed those lips between his fingers.

His cock had been abundantly enlarged and pressed considerably against his own remaining garb. His glans protruded slightly from his waistband. A clear, glistening drop formed, hung and then oozed from his throbbing mushroom capped organ.

He shoved his dance trousers down only to his ankles in his demanding hurry and his cock had sprung large formed and fully loaded into midair. He drove it upon her. She was not at all reluctant to have that done to her. She grabbed for his huge and huge-thudding prong with both hands encircling it; guiding his marvelous tool into her opening. That sensation, that first gloved contact, caused them to groan in unison.

He pumped her and leaned down to her arched and tender neck. He smelled, felt, and tasted her beauty as she surrendered to him. He kissed her neck delicately but her surrender goaded him into frenzy beyond his control.

This quick reverie was interrupted when Amanda spiked him a dark and unruly glance.

He had to go to her.

Chapter 3

HALF STORY

A spreading and soothing wave subtly expanded through her midsection as he lightly gripped her there. And then this, combined with the sensitive words and nearly nonexistent, undulating brush of his breath into her ear, eased her into a particularly contented space.

Once he had neutralized her uncharacteristically brooding moment, Marius walked the line of his performers.

Amanda happily returned to her reflections upon old Germany.

She and Giselle were solidly, if not perfectly, enmeshed; Amanda joyfully thanked her gods, though, that her lover was the antithesis of Giselle's lover. And, yes, Albrecht, ne Loys, laid abrupt claim to Giselle's full panoply of emotions. His flirtations as an inexplicably refined peasant stirred Giselle's fundaments. He stripped her of her reason, judgment and strength within hours of their initial meeting. She was absolutely smitten and beguiled. She yielded to his every affectation and, at interaction's end, fainted into his strapping arms.

How incomprehensible but also how daring of Giselle to trust to such a heightened degree that she could hand her vulnerability so swiftly and completely over to another, Amanda cogitated. How was she able? Why was she even so inclined? What was her choice of partner bound to lead her to?

As was virtuous preparation for an actress, Amanda, of course, understood the outcome for Giselle but had to pretend not to be aware. The trick for any stage artist was to emit lack of foresight in spite of having total realization of the plot from initiation to close. She identified so highly with Giselle that Amanda was capable of inserting herself into Giselle's frame at any point in the narrative; thus her divining of the uniqueness of Giselle's love for Loys. But woe to all with such power to share their core as entirely as Giselle did.

Once decided upon, Giselle was as headstrong as Amanda. Giselle had resolved that her spirit was now in Loy's possession. When Hilarion, faithful games keeper who was genuinely captivated by Giselle's essence, attempted to caution Giselle, well, she rejected his words harshly and without reserve. His intent was obvious to Giselle. He was baldly jealous of Loys and argued all cases against him. Wisely she felt, she dismissed Hilarion without regard.

Stubborn woman Giselle was, she searched out Loys and danced a love duet with him. That flaunted love was performed mockingly before Hilarion as well. The games keeper was crushed utterly; even more so as he witnessed Giselle's further cruelty when she tugged at daisy petals from a flower and the results supposedly signified Loys thorough sincerity.

Ha! So much for divinations and foolish rituals Amanda silently scoffed.

Hilarion's torture from the spectacle was mercifully ended when Berthe escorted her daughter through their door in trepidation over Giselle's condition.

Loys heard horns at this point and figured that those blaring sounds preceded his soon to be father-in-law's hunting party. A timely disappearance was in order for Loys. So he retreated well out of anyone's sight.

Engrossed in the tale, Amanda continued spinning it out in her mind. She sifted amidst those occasional behaviors of Giselle's that Amanda disagreed with or disapproved of. Her wickedness in front of Hilarion was certainly one of those.

Giselle extricated herself from the dutiful and anxious Berthe and sped out in impulsive urgency to further merge in the ongoing festivities.

Bathilde rode side by side with her father. Amanda chuckled over Loys's fortunate vanishing.

His absence was short-lived; just as long lasting as the hounds and riders of the Prince and his daughter remained. Their departure signaled Loys back to the magnetic Giselle where the two danced and whirled nonstop. Berthe viewed fearfully, ever praying that Giselle survived her exertions.

Entranced by Loys, Giselle ignored the return of Hilarion who was bent upon revenge and recovering his lost pride.

He had rampaged into and through Loys's cottage and discovered that Loys was a charlatan. Hilarion brandished the Duke's sword, found laughably in the peasants abode. He blew on the nobleman's horn which had laid alongside the gleaming sword. The careless Duke had not even attempted to hide his much known accoutrements he was so sure of himself.

As Hilarion trumpeted clarion calls from the horn, Prince Courland, Bathilde and the others returned apace.

Amanda's pulse accelerated as disastrous events were poised and ready to surge, annihilating Giselle's hopes. Amanda cringed as she considered imminent crescendo for Giselle.

The Prince gawked as Hilarion passed to him Duke Albrecht's identifying instruments. He studied the items so briefly. Recognition registered with full force.

Amanda barely mouthed the Prince's query to Hilarion. "Where were these found?"

The games keeper gladly pronounced that he had pinched them from Loys's small hut. Loys was an imposter; a sham for all to see and the Duke in reality.

As expected, drama accelerated and stormed down. The Duke knelt in shame and devastation.

Giselle heard all, watched all and clasped hands over her throbbing chest where pain leapt. She wrenched the sword from the shocked Prince and advanced the blade to her hammering heart. Before she managed to pierce her own flesh, her thumping organ shattered into irregular beats whereupon Giselle collapsed into the solace of death.

Moisture built at Amanda's wide and wonderful eyes.

Giselle was to be reborn in the second act; tragically yet heroically.

Marius's voice intruded of a sudden. He clapped and barked that rehearsal was to commence without delay.

She surreptitiously wiped the forming tear aside and then stopped, stood and readied herself for his instructions.

Chapter 4

COMPLETION

Amanda was dissatisfied with the rehearsal. She recognized that, in spite of Marius's disappointment with her just completed routine, he was about to inject information in order to apprise her of more intricate details of Giselle and Giselle's behavior; thus Amanda, by sheer force of greater knowledge, next practice, was more likely to be authentic and more truly Giselle.

She had been distracted tonight though. Thoughts continued to conspire against her as she progressed through the scenes. Act Two was especially intricate and difficult for her besides because by then she felt his disapproval of her characterization and what should have been a smoothly flowing performance. He had resisted raising his voice to her but his directions branded even greater burn as he maintained level tones.

She was not capable of dismissing yet the emotional jolt that had set her mind on the unfair path of comparing Marius to all men. He was not all men even remotely. She was searching for reasons now to create discord between them.

Why was she proceeding in this manner? Perfect trust seemed predictably illusive for her. Yet, he had done nothing that served this momentary mistrust of hers.

She had not dwelt before on this subject regarding him. And that was as it should be she acknowledged to herself. She was being petulant and over reactive to that beast, Loys. Loys was fiction and so were her concerns. Let it be enough now as it was time to set these particular worries aside.

She tuned into Marius's words again.

"Amanda, to recreate Giselle as a wraith is extraordinarily difficult. It is a monumental task for any actress, any dancer, and any singer. This extra challenge must be accomplished via multiple means. You need to execute in the ghostliest of styles. Move delicately, almost as if you shimmer and are but scarcely visible. Move wistfully, as if you float and wish that you were elsewhere. Move with flexion, as if you are continuously shrinking.

Let me review Act Two with you again. Let my view of it incite you. You will be magnificent and so very proud of yourself.

Amanda spoke, "I need to hear you tell me of Giselle upon arising from her grave and her ability to continue in spite of her overwhelming sadness!"

She observed Marius smile as they sat side by side on his tan-toned giving leather couch. He was relaxed and comfortable she appreciated as he allowed himself to sink into the pleasant padding.

A flame was blazing from a stone fireplace neatly near them. They were warmed by that; and by their proximity to one another as well.

"Moonlit glade shines upon Giselle's grave. That grave is singly glowing and the moon itself has a mind of its own; and that mind focuses on Giselle exclusively. So, her grave, no other grave in the surround, gives off light.

Hilarion weeps inconsolably at the fact of Giselle's death. He is distraught and grieving as he has never been before.

He is startled and frightened suddenly. Strange emanations rise from the earth. You know them, Amanda; he does not except by legend. The legend is that these dark creatures are Wilis, female shells who, jilted before their wedding day, seep upward from their own graves at night and seek revenge upon men by dancing them to their demise. Hilarion wisely hastens away!"

Amanda interjected, "Here then, I begin my part as these beings summon Giselle from her eternal sodden chamber. Stir me Marius; teach me, infuse me! More of your renditions please. I want to be superb in this!"

"Strangely, once Giselle has been greeted by the Wilis, they depart. You as Giselle, are starkly alone, a spirit; and you are very aware that is all that you can ever be. Ooze silent lamentations here. Speak that fully in your every maneuver and expression.

Albrecht enters. He searches for her burial site. Giselle so silently approaches him. He hears her not. Then she fronts him. He is immediately upon his bent knee and tremulously pleading for her love and forgiveness.

This is when Giselle transforms, relents, and articulates her love for him. The two of them dance together. You, Amanda, and certainly in this scene, may seem to take on solidity. Giselle is happy, even rapturous. That sense fills her up completely. She grows, swells with her emotions and seems ghostly no more; until she retreats back into the forest. She becomes contracted again and you must reveal that to the audience.

Hilarion has not made his escape sufficiently, it seems. Good man that he is, the Wilis take him, whirl him around over and over and then drown him in a nearby lake. No real justice seems to come this man's way for heaven's sake. No man wants to be given the wilis!

These demons surround Albrecht equally. As one would expect of a slightly immoral man, Albrecht shows less courage than he ought and begs dramatically for his life. They refuse him, of course. They dance him and dance him through those dark hours.

Now Giselle again rises to protect her desired one before he is prostrate, exhausted and done in due to the endless forced capering. Giselle is vividly strong again. Show that strength Amanda! Exert yourself! Drive yourself against these evil ones! Have that power of mind and movement. This is not a scene to pull into yourself whatsoever.

Giselle saves Albrecht therefore. Daybreak appears, the phantoms retreat and Giselle has bestowed life upon her once lover. She has been wonderful. She did not betray herself by allying with the Wili's in revenge, vengeance or hatred of men, of Albrecht. She has succumbed not to those baser instincts! She has vanquished the Wilis as well.

Finally, you find that calmness and absolute tranquility that Giselle surely feels as she returns to her final resting place. Discover that ease at the conclusion of all that you do in this ballet, Amanda! You can and you must manage that!"

Amanda felt inspired! She was certain that tomorrow eve's repeat of Giselle would be splendid and would far excel tonight's

Chapter 5

PASSION PLAY

Marius had always preferred a simple form of communication, an Asian invention, known as haiku. It was clear, quick and, if effect was achieved, tended to contain beauty that he found nowhere else. It was poetry distilled down to the simplicity of one grain of sand upon an entire shore.

Several haikus of his own creation came to his mind as he finished his explanation and exhortation to Amanda. He was modest enough to be cognizant that his haikus did not resonate in highest quality for all; but they jumped from his heart whenever Amanda sprang to his attention . . . which was often.

Take, "The wind whispering, sensual gifts of the dance, passion into love." Or, "Dream awakening, play of light on tender hearts. Love is known fully." Or further, "Rivers of red heat, volcanic flow upon us. Bound by erupting love."

Those were his true sentiments towards the amazing and delightful creature that nestled at his side; she fit perfectly with much of what he considered his hearth and home. His love for her was real, palpable, moving He yielded to it on most occasions; obstructed only on one regular occasion.

Their own passion play was about to commence as he had resisted her tonight enough. He wanted her immediately and he read the same from her.

She turned her head to him winsomely then, as if perceiving his very thoughts, and he detected her fragile labor of breath; her excitement and desire was definitely stamped all over her look and posture.

He leaned into her mildly trembling and inviting lips. He gently placed his hand beneath her chin and insured that interlocking, fine contact remain as their tongues met softly between now open mouths.

Marius noted, he was noting very little at this point, her flying fingers opened all upper garments and then she stripped them off all while their lips remained linked. She was almost frantic but suddenly drew back from him and then stood before him.

She moved her hips subtly and sensuously. He was complete captive to her brazen stare and delicious sway.

He spread his clothed legs to more greatly enjoy his cock climb toward her; material of his jeans strained at this. He rubbed that area through the material but was transfixed and did not release his bulging tool for the moment.

She continued to pose for him hotly. Amanda was built uniquely for a svelte and lean woman. Her unique attributes were no longer hidden by a laced cornflower blue full bra.

These beautifully pendulous and largely mounded breasts of hers caused his cock to jerk a bit beneath his zipper.

One of many reasons he cherished their lovemaking was because he got to lay his eyes upon, taste, and touch these otherwise tightly bound assets of hers especially restrained during all dance routines. The audience expected bust-less heroines. And they were entitled to have their expectations met.

He, however, was absolutely mesmerized by her genuine nude physique. He thought of only one other in the profession busty as Amanda was.

Her breasts hung magnificently before him. That quality of size by itself was enough. But it was not all. Her bulging curves there exposed the faintest venous mapping that flowed to aureoles; those aureoles pink and big around as would be a demitasse saucer. Thick, darker brown straining nipples begged for him to approach her. And his member was becoming too thick. He would approach her as soon as he released himself from his clothing.

Marius closed the distance between them once his pants had been peeled off and tossed aside.

He knelt before her as she curled over his head simultaneously. He cupped her breasts with both hands and sucked greedily at her hardened nipple. The plump flesh against his tongue roused his organ to its utmost size quickly.

Amanda's uncontrolled light moans and her extended arm and clutching hand to his cock brought him to a very dazed point. She fisted him there, squeezed powerfully to force his mushroom shaped head to enlarge and redden intensively and then released in a rhythm Marius found irresistible.

Marius stopped and rose up to his complete height then; lifting Amanda gently upward to do the same.

After, Marius dropped a finger to his throbbing cock and removed a silken, clear dew drop from his opening. The drop was tiny; reflective of his immense desire for her. He carefully ran his lubricant over her scarlet lips and she slowly tongued over those lips gladly. She shivered in pleasure.

He drew his several fingers to her juncture and traced from top to bottom. Meanwhile, they just gazed at one another; pretense that nothing was happening below elevated the pleasure vastly.

She was paralyzed.

He kissed down to her turgid, fattened nipples again. Yet this was only a mere beginning for him. His mouth traveled intently lower over her superheated, blushing flesh.

Suddenly, she freed herself from her rigid stance. She pulled at his straight and long hair, stepped back slightly, gentled herself up against the walls hard surface, sank down upon his mouth ever so minutely while she pushed his head hard into her clit and cleft and then held her wide expanse of breast with one hand and grasped, squeezed, then thumb stroked her tip.

He pressed her flesh at nether lips high and wide with his flattened palms so that her lips were separated especially for clitoral prominence and exposure. He encircled that tender knot and sucked it in. He proceeded to alternate his tongue between licking vertically and lashing horizontally.

Amanda panted and trembled through his ministrations.

When her legs began to quiver, he intensified his assault upon her. His left hand caressed her thigh and his right hand finger-pumped her hugely responding vault.

His tempo was strong and rapid. She moaned and then cried, "My love, my love."

Her contractions rushed into his mouth and shattered her poise irrevocably into raging, engulfing ecstasy.

She swooned against the wall and Marius slid his chest up her body and caught her before she fell.

In spite of her blissful collapse, he commanded her to wrap her legs around his waist. His pulsing organ lay against her Venus mound.

He swiveled, and she was carried by him, into a chair of his; deep-set with thick wood arms. He sat first, she atop him and they were positioned face to face. His massive and yearning tube penetrated her in a hardly noticed instant.

Marius was up to her hilt. Amanda was weak but roused by his entry into her. She gushed out fluids for him. She balanced herself by putting her hands to the oaken chair arms. He caressed her ass cheeks.

He wanted release fiercely. He stroked into her a fraction. She had to have his release also and returned his stroke. He removed his hands from her buttocks and clamped them over her wrists. She was constrained and that rapidly incited her.

She pumped him almost brutally, fast and took everything he had to give and pounded upon him. The beautiful scald of it created panting groans from both.

Marius felt her sweet bludgeoning of his manhood to his core. She must have experienced it to an extreme also. Suddenly she spasmed forward, her forehead braced between his pectorals. She lolled there as she experienced echoing waves of release synchronized with his. Jet after jet of come sprayed upon her insides.

They trembled together in their aftermath.

Yet he was desperate to part from her.

And she was shocked and dismayed. He was capable of sensing that but was even more quietly frantic to have her leave him and leave him immediately regardless of her reaction to what must have seemed very callous.

Chapter 6

DEFINITE PAUSE

His behavior toward her had been blatant and greatly concerning to Amanda. It had caused her to definitely pause; having been a more easily dismissed notion earlier. Valerie's presence indicated Amanda's obvious concern.

Valerie gently remarked to Amanda, "I have seen you this deeply upset only once before. Do your instincts say to you that his treatment of you is as significant as that asshole Ramone's was? Tell me no. I have more regard than that for Marius!"

Amanda flinched slightly.

"I am so sorry sweetie. I just find it perplexing that Marius would be obtuse enough to scorn your love and risk what is such a beautiful connection between the two of you. You are beyond being a jewel Manda; you are an exceptionally flawless diamond."

When Amanda was lost and forlorn, as she was presently, her steadfast and remarkably supportive friend, Valerie, was whom she called upon. They had been pals since preschool days. Amanda trusted her judgment and wisdom implicitly. Even in discord, they found the avenue which led them to that compromise allowing for both learning and their further deep attachment. Amanda relied on Valerie equal to, more usually, than any man that Amanda had ever met or contemplated bonding to.

Amanda would have confided in her parents but her shame prevented her. Revealing possible errors to her mother and father, and they would not have approved her intimacies with Marius as they did not approve of Marius at all, was not a route that she wished to consider for the time being.

Also, Valerie had witnessed Amanda's near emotional dissolution when her initiation into intimacy had terminated in disaster. Amanda and Valerie had been in their late teens when that first lover of hers had been discovered a cheat. This partner, Ramone, had befriended and then seduced a dance peer of Amanda's. In a spat with Amanda, this woman had boasted of intercourse with Ramone. Amanda had been crushed and held no fellow dancer as friend from that moment forward.

Amanda recognized that Valerie had never been interested in the arts. Thank god was Amanda's reaction there; the competition had never been missed. Valerie's forte was in sales and management. She had sold payrolls to small businesses but now acted as manager of a coterie of those same sales people she had formerly been. Artistry existed in that occupation but certainly not conventionally considered as such.

Then, as Amanda went into meltdown, Valerie had sat in Amanda's kitchen nook with an arm slung over Amanda's shoulder. As Amanda wept more, Valerie drew her closer and murmured, "Honey, honey, I am here for you."

"I am so confused," Amanda rasped out between choked breaths. She alternately gasped for air and attempted to spit out words that became garbled and unintelligible.

Amanda attempted more, "He loves me, I know. He made such, such beautiful . . ." She dissolved into more body shaking sobs and was unable to verbalize the end of the statement.

Amanda shuddered and was absolutely defenseless against her emotions. She knew that she would calm as she leaned into Valerie's comforting hug.

Valerie tilted her head and rested her cheek against Amanda's hair and soothed Amanda with an almost unconscious consoling rub at her scapula.

Amanda's muscle tension eased and she successfully attempted her prior unfinished statement. "We had just made such beautiful love.

How could he have rushed me from his living room? He insisted that I get dressed without hesitation. He watched intently as I nervously replaced my attire. His impatience was so obvious. He almost threw my jacket on me and hustled me to his door. He pecked me on my neck as he then turned and closed his entrance on me. It was definite, certain and impossible to misinterpret. He required my abrupt exit! But why, I wonder why?"

Valerie started slowly. "You have mentioned to me periodically that, especially as the hour becomes late, he has insisted that you cannot stay overnight with him in his abode. Correct?"

Amanda did not reply. Her frown though gave Valerie all the answer that she needed.

"That has not seemed peculiar to you before this incident?"

"Not really, Val. I am always inclined to give my loved ones the benefit of the doubt. I also allow for people's idiosyncrasies. I love my open-minded qualities and practice that trait frequently. You know that."

"I do know that and have always cautioned you to not bend and yield excessively. You become victim too often in that manner.

Is it idiosyncratic behavior of his or is Marius being excessively surreptitious? And if the latter, what becomes the transparent answer? I do not want to alarm you but if I did not suggest that he may have another lover I would consider myself negligent as a friend to you. And our connection means so much to me.

Think! Is there other patterns of his that might support my doubt of him? Hmmm, think carefully here. If it is so, you are much better off recognizing his rude and cruel approach now, yesterday even!"

Amanda protested. "I . . . . love . . . . him!"

Valerie sighed heavily. "Yes, you are lovely in your loyalty and hope for the best. But your idealism has caused you severe pain those few years ago.

So let me make a suggestion, Manda. Do you all gather at the studio tomorrow evening?"

Amanda blurted, "He is absent so much of the day until rehearsal. He never chooses to accompany me morning, midday or afternoon!"

"To me Manda, that speaks to many negative prospects. Besides having another paramour, he could be married and his wife works at night and arrives home in the day. Maybe she even travels and appears erratically. When she arrives, Marius insists upon your departure.

Let me continue my suggestion. When all are away, I will enter his house and search the premises thoroughly and without leaving a trace of my having been there. Do you have a way in?"

There was a definite pause. Amanda let another tear fall. "Unknown to Marius, I do. I took one of his extra keys once, copied and then replaced it. I am ashamed to admit that I did this. I needed the reassurance, with or without his permission, that I had access to him at all times if necessary."

Valerie insisted, "Hand over that key."

As Amanda gave Valerie the key, she insisted, "Be careful Val!"

Chapter 7
TICK TOCK

It was eerie as Valerie walked the concrete path up to the front entry. The house, the neighborhood, was fog enshrouded as was so common when homes perched on waterfront property overlooking the Sound. A cool and moist atmosphere was the norm in middle Fall as it was currently. The heavy mist served her existing purposes well even if she was a bit frightened by the spooky vibe it gave to her. Thankfully though, Marius's porch light shone vividly through the murky white.

Valerie had the key ready to use from the moment she exited her parked car. She had felt the cold thoroughly as she quietly paced from around the block to his steps. She mildly shivered at the coalescing of the outdoor temperature and her nervous edge creeping in ever widening circles within her gut and chest. Anticipation was obviously kept in check but would not completely abate as Valerie wished.

The key solidly fit into place. Easy that she smiled. Valerie turned it firmly and it silently moved for her. With knob twisted, she pulled back on the door. It did not budge.

Oh my god Valerie thought. Of course, as she peered at the area, she spied the nearly concealed inset deadbolt; there would be two devices and two keys necessary to pass inside. Foolishness flooded over her completely. She gazed at the deadbolt in pure frustration.

She almost decided to circle the structure to check for entry otherwise but instantly realized the folly of that approach. That was precisely the action that would arouse utmost suspicion by neighbors. What then? She was certain that Amanda's lover was being neither true nor honest with her wonderful friend. Damn if she would fail Amanda again. She had always despised Ramone and had botched warning her off the bastard until it was too late!

Valerie performed the last option available to her. And it had almost zero probability of success. She snapped the key from below, inserted it above, applied pressure and, miraculously, it affected the deadbolt. The release thudded softly yet clearly and the door fell open a fraction. Valerie stepped in.

As she did this, she surmised that Marius supposed it would not occur to anyone to attempt the same key in both locks. That just simply was not the convention. He counted on inside the box thinking only. He had grossly underestimated how significantly gross desperation could force one's thinking outside of the box.

She strode through to the living room.

She was fortunate in that his decoration was spare as could be. A masculine style applied to his interior aesthetics. Even his wall-hangings were minimal to nonexistent. This room was overshadowed by four elements and no more. One wall was an immense fireplace without a single brick. Natural huge chunks of stone formed the frame for the cavern like fireplace hole. A mantle brow without anything upon it except an antique clock swept into the rugged rock and over the uniquely round shaped opening. That was element one. A huge leather couch was the second. But it did not dwarf the window wall that it was positioned under. This was the manner by which the panorama of often wind whipped Puget Sound water was observed and much appreciated. Wild weather permeated waterway after island after waterway and added that final breathtaking aspect. Craggy peaks, deeply snow covered due to excessive recent precipitation, loomed beautifully at a fair distance even in nights dark. Amazing, was Valerie's reaction.

Valerie caught herself lingering. Search girl, search! Obsessively though, she ran through the final element. It was a rustic, primitively hewn, knurled oak, lushly padded prominent chair. That chair settled in solidly with the dark toned carpet.

It was time that she applied organization of her thoughts to her foray for signs.

Nothing was apparent in this space once she looked behind the couch and underneath it and then the chair cushions.

She wheeled into the bedroom where she hoped to find notoriously personal clues. She carefully sifted through drawers, underneath the brand new bed, into closets with clothing pockets consistently empty. His shoes were in precise order and did not assist her whatsoever.

She marched into bathrooms, a recreation room, and a quick scan of the gleaming and seemingly hardly used kitchen. She assumed that most men did not cook anyhow. The refrigerator and shelves were packed; neatly and with the vaguest layer of dust upon the various packages.

She was shocked. She came upon no journals, letters, rings, flotsam and jetsam that would point her the way toward proof of Marius's duplicity.

Well, Valerie was prepared to retreat and planned on relenting. She was incorrect in her negative assumptions of Marius. Maybe he simply had weird habits that were innocent and not worth emphasizing or stressing.

She leaned on the mantel to catch a last breath. The tick tock of the clock morphed into chimes as the precise hour was marked off. Valerie loved the sound and was drawn to it.

The slender edges of the clock caused her to take a fleeting glimpse in at the device and pendulum within. Clocks fascinated her. At their surface, the device appeared to have virtually no complexity at all. How incorrect that assumption was.

The glass front had delicate gold and black filigree expertly applied to the bottom corners. She leaned her head in to more appreciate the quality of the painted design.

She jerked her head back. She squeezed the clasp at the instruments side, close to that artwork upon the glass. The clock door popped open a hair. She reached in and stilled the movement of the pendulum.

A moment ago, as she peered at the design, behind that design, as the pendulum swung, there was a faintly strange color reflected off the interior cherry wood surface; a color that was not supposed to be there.

Her fingers gently peeled a photograph from the pendulum's posterior.

The small rectangular print was of an astoundingly gorgeous woman. The written script, the inscription beneath, was in a foreign language.

Amanda must be shown this.

Chapter 8

FRACTURE LINE

Marius had seen Amanda to the hospital the very eve that his house was being intimately surveyed by Valerie.

Amanda had completed her warm-ups and had excelled at transforming herself into Giselle as Marius had elucidated to her so gracefully before their lovemaking. But then she had buckled over onto her knees with a grimace etched into her face. She tore at her slipper and attempted to yank it off. It was then that she groaned and pleaded to be attended to.

Her foot ached and shot periodic needle sharp jabs into the very center of that foot she told Marius.

Without missing a beat, Marius called emergency dispatch and sirens were heard within minutes. The medics dispensed with their copious questioning as Marius shepherded them quickly through the description of events. They lifted her to the gurney, covered and secured her with slight elevation and applied ice to the affected foot. She was propelled away with superb efficiency then.

Marius followed the ambulance in his auto. Surprisingly, he kept up with the fleeting vehicle. He veered away once he observed them trundle her into the emergency room itself.

He was certain that the constant percussive pressure of the dance had finally gone beyond the tolerance of her bones and she had suddenly developed a stress fracture, a shallow fracture line, in one or some of her metatarsals. It, unfortunately, was a common occurrence in ballet. The almost sheer slippers provided an absolute minimum of protection for the most vital body part needed for any ballet. He might have been exaggerating some here as the voice and brain were at least as important as the feet. Further, even when the foot was ace or otherwise additionally wrapped, the bones still often yielded and cracked.

Amanda's understudy, her second was now to substitute as Amanda would have little choice but to go through the progressive levels of orthopedic rehabilitation and early bouts of physical therapy. Depending upon the severity of the injury, which only X-ray would disclose, a cast would even be a consideration.

Marius bemoaned her loss. He loved her and was devastated by her agony; even if not entirely shocked at the potentially inevitable happenstance. He also regretted her absence from Giselle, although that was so secondary. And he perceived that she would choose to stay at her parents where he was thoroughly unwelcome.

It was certain. He would not go there and therefore, he would not see her again for a month, conceivably more.

He missed her already and was distraught at the idea of reliance upon the understudy as well. Amanda had been as perfect for the part of Giselle as there ever would be. Her second was beautiful almost identically to Amanda, genuinely talented and satisfied the heroine's role well; but not perfectly. She did not have the same luster and light that emanated from Amanda's glowing countenance.

He was an emotional wreck. He craved Amanda intensely. The ballet was to survive. The question pounding in his heart was, would he?

He automatically steered his Mercedes in the direction of downtown. He had to settle and calm himself and hoped that was to ease his throbbing head and lurching gut.

He had to have something to drink. He must quell the pulse licking through his innards. His entire physical being was knotted in distress and hurt.

He drove harder, faster; sailed through intersections and lights. He floated past crowds of ever mobile traffic and pedestrians. The Belltown denizens were dressed to kill and were partying with relish and vigor.

His haunt was before him. He was upon very familiar terrain now. He halted the shimmering and spotless vehicle once he had maneuvered it into a safe position within a safe location and exited the damn thing. He depressed his remote and strode from the area rapidly as his black car merged with the midnight shadows.

At the bar, he nursed his drink as if it was so precious that to imbibe was to waste something inexplicably unique. He pretended that the amber color fascinated him no end. Very slowly, he spun the glass round and round as he scrutinized the massed and sweaty mob clawing their way to a roused and falsely good time.

Soon enough, as he was incapable of waiting longer, he drifted into the field of cars huddled in row after row outside this always present lair. It was ever trendy, noisy, and full of drunken men and women at this advanced hour.

Marius was even surprised that any of these revelers were capable of identifying their rides. Some were hardly able to stand upright. Few followed the socially correct rule of having one amongst them remain sober in order to have a benign adventure home. The drunk and disorderly were a very sad bunch indeed.

He sidled up to one of the few who staggered from the belly of the beast, the bar, on his own. Marius feigned drunkenness himself and casually draped an arm around the amiable acting, woozy behaving, and fine figure of a gentleman. Looped yes, but a gentleman as well, Marius smirked to himself.

This fellow looked slightly askance at Marius and then chuckled briefly. He managed to slur out, "A good evening for drunks, eh?"

Marius happily parlayed with, "You are so surely right, my friend."

And they leaned in together; dark silhouettes of one head snaking in toward the other.

A deft stroke, a tiny emitted cry, vague liquid rhythmic resonances followed, both forms descended from view between the metal husks. The air then churned and an outline withdrew into night's unseen horizon.

If there had been a witness to the event, would they assume that their inebriated imagination was at play? Definitely, yes. So the frightening odds were that any random onlooker was likely to cast aside doubts, ignore all and stroll away, sloshed and unconcerned.

He banked on the fact of that human reflex.

Chapter 9

Rank Plans

Amanda had been in her mom and dad's house for a week now. She had been diagnosed with a hairline stress fracture of her third and possibly fourth metatarsal. Theoretically, she was privy to all the potential injuries and their symptoms from improper use of the various limbs. As a dancer, she had to know how to take care of herself.

But for god's sake, how was it that such a miniscule break actually caused such gross swelling and throbbing?

Amanda had been pleased that the hospital physician had never proposed a walking cast for her. The injury's extent did not merit such an extreme approach. But it did merit the doctor's outline of elevation, ice, nonsteroidal anti-inflammatory medication three times a day as a large precautionary initial dose and zero weight bearing for her for at least a week.

The week was up. And she was fed up. She did not tolerate weaknesses gladly or passively. It made her feel trapped, confined, impatient and angry; most of all angry.

Her mom, Betty, and Valerie both rushed towards Amanda as she roughly shoved her chair from her sore sitting butt, slapped her crutches aside and stood up gingerly.

She bent to speak at her disabled appendage and, from clenched teeth, whipped out, "You, foot, will work, damn it!"

Amanda then smiled at both of her would-be rescuers. "I can do it. Do not help me!"

Her forward paces were placed cautiously. "It aches, it definitely does do that. But there are no longer any of the stabbing sensations that initially took my breath away.

Look, I only hobble some. I can weight bear now. I am ambulatory again! Hallelujah!"

Valerie interjected, "Well then, I have something that I have to tell you since you are on your way to full recovery my no-longer-debilitated friend."

She shifted her gaze to Betty then. "The timing is right as well. Her foot may hurt some still but Marius will not notice her absence. He will be so busy with his understudy."

"Ouch." Amanda exclaimed. I am not so sure that I like where this is going."

"It is not necessarily a pleasant issue, you are correct. I felt duty bound to inform Betty and she and I agree and have plans to strongly recommend to you."

Betty nodded in the affirmative. "Listen please, Manda, with your usual open mind. That is my single request here."

Valerie threw a concurring glance Betty's direction and continued. "Manda, you have been understandably preoccupied with your abrupt changes since you went to the emergency room. Now it seems as if you can focus on other subjects."

"Like what specifically?" Amanda queried.

"Like that I discovered a purposely hidden item in Marius's possession when I sought out those clues as to the whys and wherefores of his problematic behavior towards you. I have it here. It is a photograph."

Valerie removed it from her handbag and thrust it at Amanda.

Amanda returned to her chair. Betty and Valerie did likewise.

Amanda held the photograph at different angles to allow the details of the miniature portrait of a woman permeate her senses. "She is gorgeous. And the inscription at bottom here, what language is that?"

Her mom answered readily. "We were unsure, both Val and me, thinking it was either Russian or German. It would seem to be a deep expression of love in German directed at Marius. See his name there?

The most perplexing aspect is that the photograph appears of the highest current quality. But at the same time she is dressed in old fashioned ballet attire at her neckline. I wish her entire outfit was visible. The contradiction of present and past is hard to figure. And unless Marius has a line of antecedents also named Marius, your Marius has been singled out by this woman. There is something terribly wrong here even if we cannot fathom it quite!"

Valerie was not able to contain herself. "You have to explore this, my too trusting friend!"

"It seems as if I am betraying Marius by studying this issue further!"

Placing her hand at tabletop upon Amanda's wrist, her mother gently intoned, "For the sake of your heart and your eventual sanity, you must seek out Marius's motives surrounding you. Are they honorable? Are you in harm's way and are ignorant of such? What do you genuinely know of him? Fundamentally, who is he really? Protect yourself my beautiful girl."

Valerie peered at Amada's downcast eyes and lifted up her chin. She brushed Amanda's cheek affectionately with the back of her fingers. "You are a love. Be good to yourself."

Then Valerie laid out the plan. "See there, within the inscription, she names the Black Forest in English. Your mother has bought you a plane ticket to what we believe is the nearest German airport to this area. You leave within days! It is a blessing that your foot is growing stronger.

I would accompany you but my boss was not amenable to that on such short notice."

"These plans seem so rank. Marius has been nothing but tender and loving towards me. How can I, in essence, say to him, by following through on the flight and the investigation, that 'I do not have a whit of trust in you, my love?' It seems so hypocritical of me."

"My precious daughter, what if the love you are so fond of associating with Marius is false? What if it is you who loves him but he does not feel the same for you?

Your brothers, sister and father are in concurrence with Valerie and me. It is neither selfish nor unworthy to expose a possible, even probable, charlatan.

As with Valerie, your siblings cannot go either. Employers are not flexible these days it seems. And your father will not let me go. He wants you, and you alone, to learn how essential transparency is between seriously committed individuals. He believes, if you do this on your own, you will find that sense of balance that comes with vivid experience. On your own, you will never forget this lesson.

As your mother, I want your well-being. But I cannot disregard your father on this. So promise me dear child that you will be wise and take no grand chances please. Ultimately, above all else, your intact return is paramount!"

"I am capable of handling myself mother!

I will go but with many reserves. I want to believe Marius and think that my travels will prove him the honorable man that I love!"

Chapter 10

LABORING TRAVELER

She mumbled, "Marius, I am so sorry."

Then she attempted to block out the cacophony ebbing and flowing around her. She was exhausted, aching from head to left foot and that very foot had taken on the puffed up impression of an overfilled dirigible. If only that foot could drift away without consequences she thought.

She massaged her temples briefly, forced her eyelids closed, sighed profoundly and finally let her head slowly settle lower until its heavy weight bent to just above her knock kneed pose. She laced her fingers together at skull base and stretched her neck and shoulder muscles from time to time but could only urge them to elongate so far. By doing this she buried her chin in her chest and certainly appeared to others a long laboring traveler.

She had not even figured how to find her route to the appropriate luggage turnstiles.

What had they all been thinking? Thankfully, she had acquired a passport well before this unhinged trek had ever been hatched. And she did not speak, read or contemplate a word of German. She was able to count einz, vie, drie, vier, funf and sex. Or she hoped that was an accurate enough set of pronunciations to have anyone understand with a little effort on their part. Otherwise, she was simply lost in a land of meaningless noise, strange symbols and nonsensical talking heads. Her sole recourse was a small book of German translations.

Also, she was not tech-savvy and so had not brought her laptop or I pad. She shifted uncomfortably, rocked and sighed at the edge of her seat in the corridors of the Stuttgart airport.

Amanda stomped her right foot suddenly and sat up brightly. This weak, whining person was not who she was! Enough of the self-pity!

For starters, she reached into her jacket pocket, palmed and lifted the still purloined photograph into her view. The inscription had been smudged some. Valery and Amanda's mom had located a map revealing the Black Forest to be in southwestern Germany. That was why she was idling away the minutes in Stuttgart.

The inscription went like this:

> Marius,
>
> Mein Herz wird immer aus dir zu suchen.
> Wie sollte ich wissen, eine naïve waif aus
> dem isolierten Black Forest, dass du wich
> jemals geliebt so.
> Meine Calw Eltern waren so stolz auf unsere
> starke Lieba wurden sie heute noch leben.

Sie pflegen mich, neigen zu wir, ist deine
sube Liebe so erfreulich.
Mogen unsere Bindung fliegen die immer
Nacht durchtanzen.

Deepest Love, Viktoria

The script was cramped and not entirely readable to Amanda's untrained eyes. The words were crowded into a very small gap from photograph bottom to lowest paper margin. She was able to deduct certain facts though. This woman wrote in both German and English. Therefore, Marius, Viktoria's recipient, spoke those languages as well. Had Amanda ever asked Marius to say anything to her in German, he might very well have unleashed fluent sentences and paragraphs for her in that dialect.

There perhaps was a precise location written; yet between the smudge and the fact that it was written in German, she had no real idea.

She put her fist to her forehead and gasped. Why had no one thought to translate the message by computer? Surely there were programs which served that purpose! And she had no access because she had no computers with her.

She could call Valerie and have her perform what would be a much easier task now!

Yet, as she was engrossed in this examination of picture and its solution, in her peripheral vision she caught someone examining her. She brushed the irritation aside. She had grown accustomed to being the object of leers, stares and all manner of fixed gazes. It was the common hazard of being female and attractive.

Of a sudden, the perpetrator, of what she deemed to be no more than a short lascivious look, approached her. She was definitely annoyed by that as she searched out her cell phone. Most of these individuals kept their distance if she just ignored the behavior.

She had no patience presently and planned on politely squashing his persistence.

He did have an unassuming and friendly smile for her though. That softened her a bit. She had an inability to turn away anyone with a kind and warm demeanor, especially in such an alien place.

Also, she was aware that any overture on his part that was not in English was to be futile.

She was about to discover his motives as he breezily sat beside her.

Chapter 11
HESITATION'S VERGE

In a very refreshingly straightforward manner, he sought to genuinely rescue her from her plight. "I can offer you help and assistance if you wish. Your obvious misery and the foreigner's book of translations gave you away. You have had a lengthy trip and are not familiar with the language. Again, may I be of some service to you?"

Amanda was relieved and overjoyed that, even if not his native tongue, he conversed fluidly in English. She grinned from that fact only.

The youngish man misinterpreted the grin as ready assent to his gesture of aid and introduced himself, "I am Jürgen. And you are . . . . ?"

Amanda paused, laughed openly and took his proffered hand. "I am Amanda."

"And what does your laughter imply?"

"That I rarely trust an unknown male this quickly. Yielding to my predicament though and opening this conversation caused my laughter. It is so unlike me that I did have to laugh at the surprise.

If it seemed rude or offensive, I apologize."

"Do not allow it to concern you. All of your variations on a smile are very engaging. But I am not at your elbow to be just complimentary. Do say yes that I can be your guide through the airport, even if no more than that."

"Would you excuse a phone call for just a moment, Jürgen?"

"But of course Amanda."

Amanda dialed Valerie with muffled excitement playing within her.

Amanda returned the phone to her purse and declared, "No answer there. I will attempt a connection again if she does not reply to my message quickly.

You do me a wonderful service. I was on the verge of hesitating and buying a return ticket and fleeing for home. Now, with your decent gesture to me, I can retrieve my luggage and carry on. You are too kind."

"I did notice you on the flight too."

Amanda rolled her eyes mildly and warmly said, "How did I know that would be the case?"

"I had a friend's marriage to attend."

Jürgen confidently took her lightly by the arm and informed her, "This direction to your belongings, ma'am.

I must confess additionally that I have an ulterior motive. Yet I will inform you of it without delay. I am a journalist and a freelance photographer. Women of a certain appearance gather my professional attention. At present, my journalistic endeavors are secondary and my photographic pursuits are primary. Presently, I specialize in portraiture and have recently developed an idea for . . ."

Amanda abruptly interrupted him in her enthusiasm. "Your skill is portraiture?! I have an item then for your scrutiny. And I have questions to ask you!"

She forgot all about her sore body and earlier lack of resolve. She meant to plumb his brain thoroughly.

"There is my luggage."

Jürgen hustled over and hoisted those suitcases from the revolving round. He was bemused. "It appears that yours are about the last collected. It is good that I am here."

"Apparently so," Amanda mouthed with soft demeanor.

"And your next step? Do you have a hotel?"

"I want to ask you those questions please. And I would also like to hear about your project which drew you to me. So, with both in mind, we need to share some hours together. Where do you stay? Do you live here or no?"

"No is the answer to that question. My residence is in Berlin but, like stewardesses and pilots, I am rarely there. My work defines my location. So, when we have the moment, I will explain my photographic effort and why I flew from Seattle to Stuttgart rather than Berlin."

"That still leaves me with an unanswered question. Do you have a hotel that you prefer in Stuttgart?"

"I do and already have a room held for me. Let's share a taxi and you should find a vacancy there too."

Amanda was comfortable with this man's air and was curious as to his professional interest in her. Mostly, she had to have him sort out the inexplicable aspects of Marius's past.

She was in no mood to divulge openly any fragment of information related to her search while in the cab. Jürgen rested comfortably next to her. His silence was satisfying and appropriate. She thought well of this man to this point.

He gained a room for her. It was not adjoined, not even on the same floor as his. She was appreciative of that as she would have had to scold him if he had attempted other. She was in love with and dedicated to Marius. Jürgen was to be apprised of that repeatedly. She was not available to anyone other than Marius in that regard. Respect and support were to be the hallmarks of her and Jürgen's sojourn together no matter how long it lasted.

She was well pleased though that having acted contrary to her instincts events were progressing smoothly and to her advantage. She was planning on being generous with Jürgen, minus the sexual, as well.

She had not received a call from Valerie. It did not matter as she had Jürgen to translate for her.

They were to dine in the hotel's restaurant in several hours. She was freshened now and went directly to his room to regale him with questions before dinner.

Chapter 12

MORE CLARITY

Dinner came, dinner went and they were yet embroiled in gaining more clarity on what was growing in fascination for Jürgen and dread for Amanda; Amanda's in her concern for recovering her security with Marius, Jürgen's in his love and pursuit of the solution to riddles of all length and breadth. Even Jürgen's project had been shunted aside, forgotten in the flurry of Amanda's exposition.

Once Amanda had laid out the known details of her love's suspicious behavior, thin and now very worrisome past and her emotional enmeshment with Marius, Jürgen had to proceed delicately with Amanda. She was there at the precipice of love's despair.

"I presume that the photograph that you were regarding with such intent when I first approached you is the very one that you must let me see now. It is the hour to put any concerns of me to rest. You have revealed your pursuit and why, now it is my turn to be proactive here. Your healthier instincts urged you to trust me. Follow those instincts further. Disclose the photograph to me please."

"I have exposed very difficult fact and sentiments to you regarding myself. My reluctance is not about trust whatsoever. Embarrassment swamps me in that I may learn that I have gravely erred in my choice of partner. So much of me does not want to go to that possibility. And the photograph is the key. Do I desire to use that key? Do I wish the truth? Honestly Jürgen, my emotional blindness felt so much better than this does."

Amanda became utterly still then. She was poised to fix on a crucial decision. Would it be the correct one? Ultimately, she realized that her own self-loathing and self-anger was to annihilate her and Marius's union if she did not proceed. She sucked in a breath, a very deep one, allowed it out forcefully and proceeded.

"Here it is. If I fail to seek out the truth, all is over anyhow."

"You are very wise, beautiful Amanda."

Amanda did not interject to begin as Jürgen studied the photograph intently.

"She is lovely, Amanda. That is a minor fact though as you are astoundingly gorgeous, surpassing her charm."

She perceived that he articulated this without guile. He was hardly conscious that he was talking as he peered at the picture.

As was automatic, Jürgen began by sorting through the inscription's translation, smudge and all its other imperfections.

"This is not difficult. I am German, its language is my first borne, the history and geography of this country are like skin to me."

Amanda gasped at her great fortune in happening upon Jürgen as he wrote out the inscription thus:

> Marius,
>
> My heart will forever
> seek out yours. How
> was I to know, a
> naïve waif from the
> Black Forest, that
> you would ever
> love me so.
> My Calw parents
> would be so
> proud of our
> strong love were
> they alive today.
> You nurture me, tend
> to me, your sweet
> love is so gratifying.
> May our bond fly the
> ever night away.
>
> Deepest Love, Viktoria

"And the smudged word is Calw. I teased that out as I know Calw to be a town in the Black Forest. Were you unaware of that fact, as most people not from Germany would be, sorting through the smudge was to have been highly problematic?"

"Thank you Jürgen. I am forever indebted to you."

"The indebtedness is mine, Amanda. Anything that will insure your greater satisfaction is my pleasure."

Amanda believed that.

"Is Calw nearby?"

"Close enough, Amanda! But there are other clues peppered here in the item. The photograph itself bares Viktoria's neckline. May I call her Viktoria? Will it disturb you if I do?"

"It will not disturb me at all my friend. If our effort is to pursue the truth to the end, then I will no longer be shy about it!"

"The clothing she wears at neckline is old fashioned. It would go back a hundred years, more probably. But how can that be so? The quality of the portrait's print is superior and I would assume can only be matched by present day printing standards.

And was she wearing the clothing in fun or as a costume? I guess not as the seriousness of her inscription implies sincerity of the photograph as well. So her clothing must be genuine also.

Did your Marius become careless and overlook the difference between photo-quality as compared to Viktoria's out of date neckline material? Did he give us a vast clue here possibly?

So how do two individuals communicate with each other, one seemingly from eighteen hundreds Germany and one living in the United States right now?

I am speculating and giving you off the cuff propositions only.

So what do you say Amanda?"

"I have no idea. It is more than disquieting; it is frightening in its many implications!"

"Not frightening yet. There has to be a rational, logical answer for this.

There is another element to this puzzle. Touch the back of the paper. It is not a smooth surface entirely. Did you notice that? Check it now and tell me your observation here."

Amanda gently rubbed the back face and was startled. She detected the faintest irregularities of its surface.

"It is a paper watermark. Studied rigorously, it yields the location of the print paper's manufacture. And it spells out 'St. Petersburg'. That is in Russia and is currently the city of Leningrad. How is it that the print paper has a watermark spelling out 'St. Petersburg' when the paper corresponds to present day standards? Shouldn't the watermark spell out 'Leningrad' then? How confusing is that?"

Amanda surprisingly stated, "I believe that we should proceed to Calw as rapidly as can be accomplished." The statement was blatantly firm and Amanda would go there.

"I must accompany you Amanda. My assistance will be invaluable to you!"

Amanda had already decided that in the affirmative. "Yes, you will accompany me."

"Briefly Amanda, allow me to explain my project to you, since we have not discussed that yet. It hopefully encompasses my taking casual portraits of you posing in the Black Forest. I knew that straightaway upon observing you. I have already wrapped five sections of Germany with five varying models to grace my flowers. It will be a coffee table compilation of photos of exquisitely appearing women holding flowers which are native to the various regions chosen. What will initially drag the prospective customer's eye to it will be the models. You and this corner of Germany are the last necessary elements for completion prior to publication. Permit me poses and postures of you with one or other buds garnished on your form. Please. That is all that I ask of you in return for my aid."

How was she to refuse? "Most certainly, that is easily accepted and may even be fun."

Why though had Valerie not called?

Chapter 13

Nightmare's Captive

Pinned and terrorized, her body trembled under the covers and she whimpered intermittently. She was dream's prisoner, nightmare's captive.

This dream had but one center and Amanda was unable to break free. It had begun pleasantly enough as dancers whirled and pranced through a wonderfully enacted Swan Lake. It was superbly accomplished and yet she had only a peripheral role in the production.

She yielded to the dream constructs as she had no other choice. And there was a shimmering, wavering quality to all that was presented from her to her dream self; it represented all that she beheld of her unruly unconscious mind. At some level of awareness, she begged not to go to fraught places. But she was not allowed escape of any kind.

Her dream gripped her. When she left the theater, the harsh chill blasted her so swiftly that she was shocked and nearly breathless. Her body tensed and it was as if she had immersed herself into some frigid, arctic lake. It was made worse by having forgotten her heavy cape inside. She pirouetted, reentered the building and became promptly lost, her bearings vanished as walls loomed, receded, blinked out of sight.

Even though she was steeped in fear, an insistent, unknown hand shoved her to the cavernous stage and its hushed perimeter. She dreaded the silence so. She was stalked by it; nearly crushed by it. Her senses heightened in an effort to detect her situation.

Then she heard peels of mocking laughter; above her, about her and lasting one time and only for seconds. The noise had ripped into her deepest innards. She was being nudged relentlessly towards an apprehension that she did not choose to be witness to. She was frozen, paralyzed, stricken. The floor beneath her feet slid river-like towards her, forcing distant objects and conditions to become immediately in front of her. A room at the end of the hallway was at her face now. She was not able to enter. Her trepidation exhausted her as well.

She was knocked inward and fell to her knees and palms. Her all fours were now solidly underneath her. How was it that her head was clasped?! Her emotions were horribly electric and a force compelled her to observe wide eyed the scene before her.

I must not see this; I do not want to see this, Amanda soundlessly screamed!

There was a master bed at her eye level. There was not a detail now which would escape her. She was incomprehensibly clamped rigidly and rendered mute. Who was this dream's cruel maestro? She was without defenses; she was starkly vulnerable and it was unbearable.

The scene unfolded clearly in the innermost shafts of her mind.

Marius and Viktoria were splayed out on the bed with remnants of ballet garb strewn about, a shred or two still upon them. Viktoria's luster was not disguised or hidden one iota. She lay supine and dared to act innocent and nonchalant. She even rolled to her belly so that her perfectly rounded twin ass cheeks and smooth ebony skin were presented to him.

He hung above her grinning at her teasing ways. He bent to kiss her tantalizing, warm and soft globes then. She wiggled and then tightened them as he laid lips to her. He ran those lips gently up her slightly elevated spinal column and then flipped her seamlessly to her back.

He gazed upon a portrait so erotic that his semisoft prod began to swell without direct touch or stimulation.

Amanda was unable to avoid observing that glistening dew drop of his; bold excitement concentrated into liquid delicateness.

He dipped to Viktoria's torso and placed his long fingers around mocha colored huge breasts. Even posing supine and with thin top remaining, her breasts massed mountainously towards him. He flicked one of her pebble sized midnight nipples with his forefinger. He drew the other of her unusually sensitive tips into his mouth. He did all of this through the material. He did not care how he took her.

Amanda hated that in this tableau. Viktoria's upper curves were slightly larger than her own curves. She also despised that Viktoria extended her arm slowly, all the while tenderly touching his nape while he suckled her, and she hefted his heavy sack and hardening length. She then deftly encircled her fingers over his red and expanding glans and the ridge at joining of shaft and cockhead. His entire organ throbbed bigger as Viktoria knew that it would. She smiled at the idea and feel of his gathering hardness.

Amanda found herself inexplicably nude now. Dream's perplexity continued as one of her hands was pressed downward. She resisted but a bit as she stared at their impassioned enfolding. Without intention, her fingers needed no further assist and she loosed them upon herself. She tapped her clit rhythmically and alternated with a slow, deliciously slippery slide between lips to her interior. Fear faded as pleasure mounted.

Marius tore at what clothing remained over his developed, solid shoulders and knelt above Viktoria. He then sent the remainder of her clothing flying. Her pendulous breasts poured even more provocatively out to him. He pinioned her wrists to the bed's surface and guided his large erection into her mouth. She lavished his hot stone piece with thorough attention as she pumped him. She did not, could not, take his complete length or girth.

Amanda was cognizant that Viktoria was attempting to swallow him whole. He was just too ample for Viktoria. It was the same for Amanda.

But what was the meaning of their old fashioned dance attire juxtaposed with the modern bed? The dream mashed it all together in a thick porridge of the rational with the irrational.

One hand of Amanda's played with her wet opening still. The remaining hand lifted one of her full breasts to her own mouth where she lashed tongue side to side over her firm tip.

Was this real?

Marius removed his cock from his loved one's lips and sank his mighty pole into her juiced entrance. He went full into her, driving fast and hard. Viktoria moaned plaintively. She finger stroked his nipples mindlessly besides.

There was an eruption of orgasm. All three burst forth with potent release.

Amanda awakened!

Chapter 14

FAVORITE ARTISTE

Rarely was there an opportunity for Marius to read and relax. Amanda's absence was not at all to his liking; it was very much a challenge to sooth himself. Edginess crept into his nervous system too frequently since her injury. Her perennial, instinctive tenderness comforted him immensely. As a substitute, he was hunkered down with a book; a book that he had read multiply, made humorous, reflective or argumentative notations scribbled in the page margins and had considered purchasing a second copy. The dog eared, thumbed through condition of this one worried him on occasion.

The content infused him, distracted him and prayed upon his thoughts. The subject of this historic read was an individual critical to the formation of modern ballet. Marius chuckled to himself as he mentally intoned, "Such a fine name, Marius."

Marius Petipa was his favorite artiste. In regards to ballet, Marius considered him the ultimate maestro. His compelling story jumped off the page and pleased Marius. This rendition of the great man was no replacement for Amanda but did manage to dial down his anxiety and excess energy until his inevitable concluding ire. He put this knowledge away for the moment though.

What interested Marius about Petipa the most? What did the author suggest were the significant aspects of his life? What of his glory? What of his exit from the adulation of his audience into an unsatisfactory retirement?

Petipa's father, Jean Petipa, was a French danseur of renown and began the son's training at age seven. The father imposed his expectations upon the younger. Marius Petipa resisted his father's rigorous demands, rebelled often but was deemed so talented that choices slammed shut on the youngster other than the proscribed path.

Marius's opinion was that generally a father's insistence upon a son bowing to the elder's demands was folly. It had worked out well in this case though. Smart kid to have pursued his natural skills with a mentor brilliant as the boy's father was. The generational antagonisms were suppressed in the interest of creative endeavor thankfully.

Father and son plied their art in France at first. Then the pair's curiosity had led them to North America. Much of their time had been spent in New York City demonstrating their skills to a rather uncultured audience. But, in spite of the disastrous production and stolen profit, the younger had been stirred by the rowdy, seemingly fearless nature of the people. Also what he had glimpsed of the natural geography outside of the city's perimeter had impressed him strongly. Here was a land to seek a home in and settle permanently. But the elder insisted upon gracing the stages of Paris again and wanted nothing to do with North America hence.

The young adult parted company from Jean when the apprentice's competence bloomed into full-fledged knack. He had an invitation from Spain's royalty to perform in the ambiance of the King's Theater.

Wonderful experience, that, for a novice, albeit an incredibly capable and devoted novice, Marius thought. What a boon at the sunrise of one's career to have abilities showcased before the King and Queen.

But then the near duel that drove him from that country permanently. Intimacy poorly selected often had dire results. Marius pictured what could have been had the younger remained there.

Marius Petipa was destined to unite with his father twice more as he abandoned Spain to be a principle danseur within the confines of France's jewel city. The lure and comfort of familiarity, additionally the rather sharp push of one cuckolded, trumped the majesty, the splendor of an enthusiastic ne loving pair of Spanish monarchs clapping fervently.

Marius pondered that there seemed a mystical sense in awing a refined audience simply by dint of aptitude alone. What a heady experience. But it was obviously not worth the younger's life.

Marius and Jean Petipa wrought beauty upon the arts of Paris again briefly at this time in their lives.

Eager and impatient to journey, the younger had arranged a contract with the St. Petersburg Imperial Theater.

The 'imperial' moniker surfaced commonly Marius observed with ironic tinge to this thought. Imperialism dominated the terrain of the day but it was in unrecognized decline simultaneously. Marius pardoned himself the veering rumination here.

Marius brought himself back into focus. Petipa was a wanderer for sure. Now he ventured into Russia. Unbeknownst to all, journey's end had arrived. Petipa was not to leave this cosmopolitan hub for the remainder of many days. His father followed suit and donated his remaining days to St. Petersburg. The father died in 1855 and the son was destined to live much longer.

His accomplishments were vast and grand while ensconced in St. Petersburg's arms. This Petipa, Marius grinned, was a rather amazing force for cultural progress. He moved upward in the ranks from principle danseur, then choreographer to premier ballet master. In addition, his creative output was inestimable. He organized and developed to successful fruition a minimum of sixty full-evening ballets. His shorter works were legion and also incomparable. Giselle was his best reproduction and he fine-tuned this marvel until it was perfectly marvelous.

Marius further read with satisfaction that Petipa quite literally constructed the foundation for modern Russian ballet by infusing it with the purity of the French form and the virtuosity of the Spanish school. Choreography was singly elevated forevermore. There were enough accolades here to bloat anyone's head.

Magnifique was Marius's sensation always upon perusing these pages. The spirit of perfect movement, high oratory, ethereal song, an actor's persuasion, and a message uplifting transformed Marius and he greatly appreciated that same inspiration of spirit in any being.

Was there a happy ending here for this consummate performer? Every surface indication resonated with a clear yes to this query of his. Well, Marius deigned, let's sift the details here. He had repeatedly gone over the text in this regard; almost each and every time that he opened it actually. This maestro had been married twice with many offspring according to the author.

And the circumstances of his retirement had been clear per history. Petipa had failed in his production of what could have been a masterpiece, the shining Magic Mirror. Ostensibly, the ballet had failed in décor and costumes. Too advanced for its times was the more likely answer here!

The summation regarding retirement and the botched quality of The Magic Mirror was insultingly pat. Marius fumed at the insult slapped upon this genius.

Flat palm smacked on book page. Was no one capable of recognizing that a new owner had no taste for quality ballet and simply desired to move the old out for the new and trendy?

The blatant unfairness was distinct to Marius. Marius flipped the Petipa volume shut and replaced it in a personal library so idly fashioned that the manifestation was that of a random assortment occasionally tended. For Marius, that was the appearance that he attempted to establish as each of the books that he possessed were actually of significance beyond question and his attachment to them was profound. But he did not opt to have that fact ascertained. A haphazard impact was all that he wished for. By all means, in that manner, those who passed through his residence were not apt to connect the recklessly strewn hardbacks with their importance to him.

Cain of Cain and Abel fame, Septimius Severus and Cinead MacAlpin were subjects of three of his especially beloved editions. The fourth individual that he was passionate regarding was Marius Petipa. That was why he was angered by Petipa's forced retirement. He was the finest of Marius's esteemed historical subjects. Petipa had contributed lovingly to his Russian audiences. He had nourished humankind's culture in manners exquisitely sensitive, finely tuned, and devotional and with vast regard for culture's furtherance.

He had shared his heart and how was he rewarded for this? This danseur aka choreographer aka master was shown the door like a pathetic nonentity who deserved nothing but the worst. Vile people, that he and his soulful contributions had been slapped aside in order to make way for the next youthful performer.

Bah, Marius reflected; is it any wonder that beings hesitate to share their skills, their dreams, and their love on a stage as precarious and unfair as that of the human stage?!

Marius had once been convinced that accolades frequently flowed without cessation to absolute madmen; individuals who had not a fleck of respect for the morals and hopes of the hoi polloi. Society after society replicated the most despicable of mob principles. And those principles discriminated against no one; all were held to its nonexistent mercy.

He understood the irony that the material contained in his library focused upon cruelty in its multiple incarnations. If studied intensively, though, his collection offered up threads of civilization's progress towards a more benevolent, more cooperative and more caring attitude. It was that more subtle context of history that moved him.

Ultimately, he desired to move viciousness aside to allow decency to preside.

Chapter 15
Downside Possibilities

Ugly, not pretty, was how Valerie genuinely reacted to Amanda's solitary send off. She especially disagreed with Amanda's father, Ray, in this regard. Valerie figured that if Amanda met with dire circumstances and did not reappear ever, no lesson was worth that heavy a risk. And a singularly beautiful woman traveling alone, even in more benign Europe, had its significant downside possibilities. Valerie was unwilling to tolerate Amanda's search of Marius's past alone and that was regardless of Amanda's conviction that she was up to the task, with or without an assist. Amanda's naiveté was breathtaking on occasion. This occasion stood out.

Also, Valerie had been the chief instigator in tipping Amanda into seriously investigating Marius's veracity of fact and emotion. Guilt washed over her overwhelmingly when she considered Amanda's wellbeing. And, good god, she did not even have rudimentary acquaintance with the German dialect. Of course, neither did Valerie but two heads were a distinct improvement over one. Cliché, cliché but true cliché nonetheless.

Based upon these considerations, Valerie had insisted that her employer release her temporarily and grant her a leave of absence. She had framed her necessity for departure as the tried and true family emergency. She had waited enough since her last request for time away and lied by stating that a suddenly ill, friendless aunt of hers required constant care for an uncertain period. Lame but her boss realized Valerie was even determined to quit if need be. She was invaluable; one of the most competent and adept sales managers that the company possessed. Of course he gave his consent.

Valerie avoided revealing her imminent departure to Amanda's parents. She did not desire having to suffer attempted dissuasion.

At the last minute, she informed Jeffrey, her husband. He understood her very legitimate concern for Amanda. They planned on frequent contact in her absence. Jeffrey became her escort to the airport and his loving demeanor was her final memory as the jet taxied away from the terminal and then exploded skyward bringing Stuttgart nearer by the minute.

As she leaned into her plush first class seat, she reminisced about the respect that she and her husband had for each other. They thoroughly supported one another and established rational, healthy compromise as necessary. Their attitude fostered a calm, non-adversarial loving accord that had endured for several years now.

Probably the most difficult of challenges that their marriage had confronted occurred early into their union. The manner in which they resolved the issue set the table for their future satisfactory concessions to one another.

Valerie recollected that she had always been highly flirtatious and content with that style. That was one reason that she and Amanda got along so fluidly. Amanda, gorgeous Amanda, picked any man and he was deliriously happy. She was not remotely threatened by Valerie's playful practices. Valerie appreciated that she was a beauty in her own right. Amanda outshone her though but Valerie was unconcerned. Her light glowed exceptionally bright and she was satisfied. Besides, Valerie never crossed certain lines. If Amanda were interested in a particular male, then Valerie, ipso facto, was not. Amanda performed invariably the same. Their profound friendship brooked no other outcome.

But Valerie realized that her musings had digressed from the original subject. And that was that Valerie and Jeffrey had discussed not only Valerie's flirtatious nature but also her determination to be intimate with men beyond Jeffrey. She was definitely not a commitment addict; commitment phobic was more correct. His beliefs were broad and she had selected him for that very reason. Jeffrey managed a pragmatism that maintained their bond and pledge to one another.

"Val my love, if we are to have any hopes of effectively navigating these churning waters; I have two very elementary conditions to propose. First, you must give me your blessing to do the same if I wish it. Last, I must remain your primary emotional object. Other intimacies will be as satellites to me. I will be the planet that these smaller satellites circle. You will never place me as lesser; nor will I give a lesser place to you. If that ever happens, we are done, you and I, with no recourse or further negotiations. Do you concede these two conditions to me?"

Valerie beamed her approval his direction.

Valerie and Jeffrey passionately engaged that night and experienced powerful sexual sensations that galvanized and fused their mutual love. Her orgasm had been ecstatic; his ejaculation had been penultimate and theirs had been blissfully simultaneous. It is odd how freedom whisks pleasure into an even greater froth. Her deliberations lingered there.

The plane's interior jolted as the jet's wheels met the tarmac. Valerie was jerked back to full present attention. There was an instant of increased gravity as the brakes exerted themselves. All slowed as the big machine maneuvered into the designated terminal slot. Valerie anticipated surprising and then meeting her friend.

The cell was at her mouth rapidly. She finally dialed Amanda's number.

Amanda answered before the second ring began.

"Val, why haven't you called me until now?"

"I am here Manda."

"You delight! You seriously mean that you are here in Stuttgart?"

"The very same city! Can you imagine? I was very concerned for you my dear Manda! A phone call did not suffice. I had to join you in your pursuit of the real Marius. You cannot say no to me now. Stuttgart and I would never forgive you!"

Both laughed joyfully.

"Jürgen and I were about to locate a rental and drive to Calw. Stay put and we will pick you up from the airport. It should take us no more than a couple of hours at the most. I will ring you at our arrival there."

"Who is Jürgen? What is Calw?"

Amanda had already severed the connection.

Chapter 16

Black Forest

Passenger seat one, backseat the other, Jürgen pointed the vehicle southwest. Amanda had excitedly introduced Jürgen to Valerie and then promptly crammed Valerie's luggage into the compact trunk and rushed Valerie into the utilitarian comfort of the rear compartment. The two eagerly caught up on events as Jürgen focused on the route out to Calw.

"It relieves me no end Manda that Jürgen is here to assist you; assist me also. Busting the language barrier was to have been a major thorn. And that was merely one of many difficulties that would have dimmed our hopes."

"I was equally relieved to lay eyes upon you my ever friend!" Amanda leaned over to Valerie, clasped her head between palms and planted several gentle kisses on Valerie's forehead.

Jürgen, as he surveyed the women's interaction, felt optimism seep into his bones. What he had witnessed up to this juncture was what he believed a connection should entail. There was obvious love, care, delight, support and a deep fine sentiment between the young women.

As Amanda informed her third on the freshly gathered details of Marius's character and how that led to a somewhat obscure town in the German Black Forest, he unconsciously guided the automobile all the while his conscious mind compared the two of them. He hated falling into this rude trap but he was powerless in the presence of such keen and devastating beauty as was theirs.

Their animation was the prominent impression of the two upon Jürgen. Energy and verve were vivid and were very contagious. He was every bit as roused to an extreme as were they and he was also confident that the threesome's fit was to be effortless and righteous in addition.

His photographic bent forced his mental process here. His reverie, therefore, went to their appearances. His fascination began with the female face. He was entranced by the light that marked Amanda there. She possessed that radiant blush constantly. It was inherent in her and was iconic in its strength. Valerie's blush was more subdued than Amanda's but was evident and distinct. Their blushes, of different quality and vigor, were scintillating on either and highlighted both women's faces wondrously.

He sighed. Just like a photographer to pay such attention to details.

In his helplessness, he continued his listing of their physical traits. Both women had lit eyes; Amanda's had a shifting concentrated blue while Valerie's were green and quite large. Both sets appealed to Jürgen intensely. He enjoyed their petite, well centered noses also. The structures, the etched angles, the flawless skin on both were classic and indisputably captivating.

Yet the hair differentiated Valerie from Amanda powerfully. Amanda's blond contrasted with the distinctly French-braided auburn locks of Valerie's. In spite of the red luster, Valerie had not a freckle on her soft and creamy skin. Possibly, he conjectured, this might have been due to the offering of a Scandinavian heritage.

When they stood, Amanda was tall and lean. Her ass was tiny. Valerie was short, minutely more rounded; although Amanda had a seemingly fuller bust. Or was it that Jürgen had not had ample time and opportunity to properly scan Valerie. He detested his sexism but was sexist nonetheless; political correctness was not his constant ally.

Regardless of his flaws, it occurred to him to suggest that they pose together for his project. These, after all, were not your ordinary beauties; they were extraordinary and exceptional.

The outskirts of Calw climbed into sight. He was impressed that an hour had already passed. The Stuttgart Airport had worked nicely for their jaunt into the little town in the forest.

"Amanda, Valerie, Calw begins to sprawl before you."

"Oh how picturesque!" Amanda exclaimed.

Valerie wiggled to her window and cried in pleasure. "The allure here is special. The houses are so neatly placed and unique, meticulous."

"I have never been to Calw but I have blundered across several facts about the hamlet in my wanderings.

Is either of you familiar with the German author Herman Hesse? His home is located here and seems to attract a plentiful number of tourists."

As October was to have it, a festival was winding to a conclusion for the day.

"We have arrived late. There are swarms of people. Jürgen, I must thank you for your booking of hotel reservations for us last night. We would be sleeping in the rental otherwise." Amanda mused.

Valerie was to squeeze in next to Amanda on the bed as only a single room had been available upon booking. Jürgen knew, lucky soul he was, that he would get the couch for his sweet dreams.

"It totally escaped me. This is the time of the fifth season for Calw. It's an annual event which has carried on since antiquity. We are in for a treat of dance, music, drinking. Uh, presuming we can spare a moment to have good times." Jürgen looked questioningly at Amanda.

"Umm, I am unsure."

"Jürgen, Manda has to emphasize Marius's trail. She has to resume her place in her Giselle soon enough too. There may be no time to linger and partake of festivities. Even your photographs might require delay." Valerie was adamant and presumed that this declaration dovetailed with Amanda's desires.

"I will be so unobtrusive when I use my camera. The floral spectacle in fields and meadows are unpredictable presently. This is my clearest chance to snap buds in the Black Forest. And I have a deadline too! Say that you, Amanda and Valerie, will grace me with the barest minimum of poses. Say yes to my proposition. Both of you please! I beg of you. I promise the bulk of my attention will be paid to your search. I want Amanda's questions answered; be assured of that!"

Amanda put a finger to her lips as she briefly turned to Valerie. Valerie quieted herself.

"Jürgen, you have already unraveled more than I could have accomplished in weeks. Yes, we will pose for you and pose happily." She smiled at Valerie.

Valerie peered downward in assent.

They parked before their quaint set of accommodations.

Chapter 17
CHECKING IT OUT

Jürgen brushed his teeth vigorously. He shut the door then for privacy.

Valerie promptly probed Amanda her early attachment to him, if any.

"It's only been over a day since he and I met. He has been a godsend and has asked virtually nothing from me, and you, except for a limited number of straightforwardly arranged photographs. He is phenomenal.

But if you choose to seduce him, I have no issue with that. We are all adults, including Jeffrey. As long as lines of communication are forthright and the involved people are content, so am I. Most significantly for me, though I am fond of Jürgen, I love Marius until details prove that I should not.

Do you find Jürgen attractive?"

"Well Manda, I do find him very appealing. His eyes arrest my attention. His intelligence peaks my interest, he has a command and confidence that is alluring and the fact that he is big and burly meets my standards pretty damn well too."

Amanda giggled slightly.

"You are bad Val. Let's see where your charm gets you with this European. You have not flirted with him yet I noticed."

"I have not had the opportunity really in the car and I probably will not need to. I will permit my body to express a language all its own tonight.

Will you be able to sleep through the sounds in these tight quarters?"

"I had a disturbing dream that wearied me last night. I managed no settled sleep. Your lecherous activities will not disturb me."

"Isn't it pleasurable to be adults?"

"You just allow him to be capable of reviving himself early tomorrow. Otherwise, your bottom will get sorely smacked!"

Their laughter sparkled with good humor and complete understanding.

The bathroom door was flung open.

"Is that laughter at my expense?"

"Of course it was not about you, mister bozo. Just lash yourself to the couch and I will make haste with the lights."

Valerie flipped the switches, shook her braids loose and tucked herself into the queen bed where Amanda sleepily resided.

"Do make a bit of room for me, lovely lady."

Amanda scooted to one side, barely conscious.

A few hours elapsed and only Jürgen's hushed respirations were heard in the well heated space.

Valerie slipped from the sheets and paused long enough to efficiently remove her pajamas. All that pressed upon her form was a sheer, red-dusted set of lacy bra and skimpy thong panties.

She was about to check Jürgen's situation out. And she was eager to do so. She had been imagining their tussle and was certain that it was about to seize each.

He was flat on his back. Valerie approved of that position for its very friendly ease of access.

She blew these words very gently, very carefully into his ear, "Do not open your eyes."

His eyes snapped open for but a blink and then snapped closed again. He was awoken, now alert, and therefore he gladly complied.

She stripped his thin blanket and standard sheet from his chest to the foot edge of the couch. He had light brown striped briefs on. She dipped a hand through the circle of material that wrapped a thigh and touched his resting cock and slightly textured sack. Both were large and delicious to stroke delicately.

She bent to his nipple and tongued his sensitive nub.

Her oral rhythms were having their definite effect; so was her delicate stroking alternating with grasping his shaft and encircling her fingers at his well-defined glans. Her hand danced upon him teasingly. She experienced his throb's acceleration and his flaccid tube's stretching; his cockhead reddened, swelled and hardened with her tactile magic.

He barely raked her slightly sleep-tangled curls.

He reached blindly to her bra-protected breasts. He thumbed her rising nipple through the material. It was seamless, smooth and her nipple was as if without barrier. This nipple was abundant and firm. He imagined its color and his cock jerked in her grasp and stiffened more.

He was somewhat taken aback. How had she hidden her size so successfully there? He had to have her remove her bra now! There was the mildest tremulousness in his voice when he requested, "Please remove your bra gorgeous. Now please."

Parted from his nipple, Valerie used her free hand to tweak the bra clasp, slide it perfectly, shake out of it with one arm and remove her other hand from him so that she was able to drop it to the carpet. Her hand snaked rapidly back into place ministering to his throbbing rod.

He laid his hand over hers tightly and pumped their dual fist hard and methodically over his pulsing, swollen flesh. He froze their motion and then squeezed strongly. Blood was trapped in him in this manner and his cock turned crimson, expanded more and ached excruciatingly.

His surprise centered upon Valerie's size. Once the cups were separated from her chest, her mounds hung broadly over him. Her breasts were exquisite; big and soft. His lust grew manifold. She dragged her tips over his tips. Then he palmed what he could of a breast and just held it. Her nipple grew against his palm's surface.

They waited no longer. He lifted his ass and she yanked at his underwear; she was desperate to embed his cock in her mouth. She straddled him backwards, the two performing a precarious and heated sixty nine on the couch.

She tasted his verge. She desired his come in her mouth, down her throat. But she was in greatest yearning that he come inside her.

He sucked greedily at her clit and spread her lips wide. He flicked his tongue into her erratically, passionately.

She moaned louder. He panted as he kept licking her unending juices.

He was to have her; immediately and prone.

He stood up from the couch quickly, guided her smoothly to lie upon her stomach.

He pulled her thong strap to the side and thrust himself into her. She muted her sob by compressing her face into a cushion. He was enough long and wide that he reached inside of her to her hilt though she was flat and not angled upward to meet him. She trembled but was otherwise passive. He clutched her rear and pistoned hard and fast.

His heavy bursts into her triggered her crashing waves. She forgot the cushion and cried momentarily as he was simultaneously paralyzed by his ejaculation.

Amanda heard it all and came soundlessly but excruciatingly strong as she too lay on her belly with both hands beneath her. Her fingers promptly ceased their relentless play upon her clit and interior, her hips stopped moving altogether once fulfillment had occurred.

Silence in the room was profound and inexorable.

Chapter 18

FINEST OF BREWS

At some moment before shafts of early dawn had brightened the shuttered blinds, Valerie had crept into her portion of the bed. She drowsed but was held short of true slumber by satisfied replays of their heady encounter. In her rather expanded involvement with the male sexual domain, she had never been pummeled from behind like that before. The juncture between her legs felt thrashed; yet remained blissfully sore in its recollection.

Therefore, sleep unwilling, Valerie became the sunrise bully whose chore was to rouse Amanda and Jürgen. They were beastly tough to arouse and they aggressively pushed her efforts away.

The sheet alone covered Jürgen to his waist. Valerie contemplated assaulting his nestled cock again to force him into some kind of action, any kind at all. But then further inaction surely was to ensue and his stubbornness would increase. She resisted kissing his sweet package then.

Amanda was resting upon her side, eyelids sealed with nary a rustle of eyelashes. Amanda murmured, "It cannot be time to rise. I am not ready. Val, please, a bit more."

Valerie, amazingly, was already showered and poised to lead them into a complete set of solutions today. She had no idea how to proceed though. The photograph was to become their tool as they attempted to further their investigation.

So, as she sat and observed her partners continued repose, she pondered Amanda's bona fides physically. The sheet and blanket neatly covered her up to the knees, no further. Valerie was bemused and bewitched. She had been perpetually in awe of Amanda's physique. Her build, simply, was ever awesome. Presently, her head rested effortlessly on her crossed forearms. Her sweet blond hair was everywhere; stranded across her forehead, seemingly tickling her cheeks, putting an impeccable frame to Amanda's soft visage and, as well, fanned out copiously down her side to her narrowed waist. A given, as a professional ballerina always had to maintain her form, was Amanda's absolutely level belly and her long and taut legs even in repose.

Glorious, Valerie deemed. And then there were the inexplicable, impressive outsize mounds that pointed their tips at Valerie presently. They rose and fell some with her comfortable intake of air. Valerie's breasts were big, bold and, yes, beautiful as well as Jürgen had discovered this morning. They were especially large-seeming on such a small person as she was. Her aureoles and nipples aroused all comers. But they seemed diminished to her in comparison to Amanda's. On each mounded and superbly pendulous breast, and Valerie studied them now without interference, was the most appealing of a glowing pale pink circle, crinkled slightly with their exposure, and a thick and naturally elongated richer hued nipple. Her breasts beckoned magnetically.

But, strangely, though Valerie loved Amanda's exquisite appearance and was certainly proud to be in Amanda's company at all times, she had never wished for their intimate entanglement. Women were objects of high aesthetics only to Valerie. She appreciated all pleasing form but she just had no compulsion to touch. It was men who stimulated her passion exclusively; Jeffrey the most, always Jeffrey. And that was even when pounded as thrillingly as Jürgen had done, Jeffrey remained her man and her husband. Her whole commitment was to him singly.

Time was upon them, Valerie realized. Permanent rise and shine for the day was imminent and unavoidable.

Bodies rushed past them as they stepped into the outdoors.

"This town is quite enchanting. But repeat Jürgen, what is being celebrated in the marketplace?"

"Every year, in October, sweet and lovely Amanda, Calw has a fair that they officially entitle the Bremen Freimarkt. Essentially, it is a two week folk festival and we have found ourselves in the midst of its downside. The concluding parade probably occurs in a day or two."

"Manda, you brought the photograph with you, yes?"

"I did Val. But I am not sure where to begin with it."

"Well, when all else fails, let's have ourselves a drink and ponder our strategy over the best dark beers in the world.

Germans understand how to hoist a beer-filled stein to their mouths better than anyone!"

Jürgen was adamant and before either of the women protested, he took their arms and led them through the central market to the Ratskeller. It was as if he had an instinct for the most raucous spot in town. Quiet strategizing did not seem to be on his mind.

Hoards of bodies were inside, almost spilling out the entrance. The three waited patiently as they drew ever closer to available tables.

At one of these precious tables, a crew of young men caught view of Amanda and Valerie. They were pleasantly blind to Jürgen's presence. They shouted out, "Come, squeeze in here. We will find a place for you." This was bellowed in German of course, so Jürgen, as usual, was a necessity.

Two of the men stood for Amanda and Valerie and offered them their chairs. Jürgen and these two remained standing. This was no longer a restaurant but had become a party house. The joyous noise resounded off the walls.

Valerie and Amanda were aware now that strategizing was not about to happen here. That required a sanely placid location, which this was definitely not. Silently they concluded that Jürgen had been a brat.

In short order then, Amanda handed Viktoria's portrait and inscription to Jürgen so that he could fashion a brief explanation and then query them a bit. He managed to do both over the din of the place.

The men paused and then started chattering amongst themselves, ignoring Jürgen. Jürgen pressed by saying, "The history of the town is crucial; or possibly the history of the Black Forest too to our pursuit. Think gentlemen, please."

Now that the men realized that the women and Jürgen were an inseparable item, these fellows were ready to have them be gone. So blithely and dismissively, one of them replied, "There is a museum in town. It should be open. Maybe you want to go find it right now." And they turned away.

Jürgen, Amanda and Valerie recognized the conversation was finished. The women returned the chairs and the three retreated from the facility without a backward glance or even a sip of the finest of brews.

Chapter 19

OLD GUY'S GIFT

Jürgen recognized without a shred of a doubt how significant the lead they had been flippantly proffered was to them. Really, to hell with those rude drunks Jürgen mustered to himself. Who cared?

The first passing couple who appeared other than a tourist to Jürgen, he asked if they knew the whereabouts of a folklorist museum here in town. As their good fortune would have it, they were kindly directed the way to what was a collection of Black Forest information tucked into one of those spotless and quaint structures that were common to Calw, the Palais Vischer.

The three of them were quite anxious to enter the building. The hours suited their very requirements and, thankfully, most of Calw was absent and out soaking up suds or sun. Euros for admission were taken by what must have been the curator as the old man was alone amongst the objects of folklore and local history.

Amanda, Valerie and Jürgen spread out into different sections of display. Principally, the museum dealt with four subjects that they were able to discern. One segment of the museum dove into the region's watchmaking industry.

Apparently, Amanda read, watchmakers past and present in the vicinity were renowned and cherished. A second corner featured a myriad of cuckoo clocks, their relics, and descriptions of the challenges of local German artisans to perfect the wonderfully crafted instruments. Valerie had no idea of their slow development into mechanisms of fine quality and a delicate regard to carving and painting the exterior. Jürgen perched above an exhibit which detailed the fabled folklore generated by the Black Forest. He scanned the various summarizations that spilled out the finely tuned tales written by the Grimm's Brothers, the deeds of Hansel and Gretel, Sleeping Beauty and a veritable trove of stories that persisted and fascinated.

All three came together in a final tiny room that was stacked with books and manuscripts, a countertop rife with what seemed to be piles of photographs, news fragments, utensils, devices; none organized for coherent perusal.

Jürgen sighed wearily. "This looks to be items connected to politics and government. It is hard to decipher anything here. But the curator can assist us. If a section in the museum is to be dedicated to these subjects, he has to have unsurpassed knowledge. And if not that, maybe he has a nugget of information of some kind."

Jürgen stepped decisively to the front nook where the older man hunched over a newspaper. A newspaper likely meant a dearth of computers existed here. He had detected none to this moment.

"Excuse me, are you the curator here?"

In German, the curator stated, "Yes I am." He nodded affirmatively as well.

"I am curious as to the state of affairs of your backroom. Is that an eventual display for the public? And am I correct in presuming that the information contained within the room regards history, politics and local government?"

"That is entirely accurate. You are very astute."

Amanda and Valerie continued to wander amongst the exhibits. They did not want to intimidate the curator and were beyond understanding the words besides.

Jürgen still possessed Viktoria's rendering and placed it in view.

Conversation became quickly energized then, especially on Jürgen's part.

After approximately a half hour of back and forth, Jürgen profusely thanked him.

Jürgen sped out and the women smiled large at the curator as they exited.

"This is marvelous. I am going to dub it the old guy's gift. He was amazing in what he revealed to me. Such good fortune for us! We stay one more night here while I tell you both everything."

Securely locked in their room in the lodge, Jürgen talked. Amanda and Valerie were riveted.

"When I placed the photograph before him, he was not instantly able to identify her. That disappointed me no end. I calculated that he was well informed on Calw's history. But then he squinted in intense concentration. A notion was about to break through. I could see that and held my breath in hope.

Did you hear it when he thumped the counter with his fist? That is when he attained quite the connection.

He expressed to me that if the disorganized room had been attended to suitably, we would have resolved the issue ourselves. In one of the piles of news cuttings, there is an image of a very striking young woman. It is on old yellowed paper and the photographic print is grainy but her handsomeness was not to be denied by quality of paper or print. That woman and Viktoria are one and the same. He was certain of it!"

Amanda squealed and Valerie squeezed her hand tightly.

"The clipping had to have been from the early to the middle eighteen hundreds he assured me. And that matches the timeframe that we have decided is accurate.

He had many items to sort through one evening, he told me. And that is when he happened upon Viktoria's clipping. Her beauty tantalized him even in his hurry. Therefore, he examined the article below it.

Apparently, Viktoria's father was a miner and there was a vein of silver that was being prospected and developed in a segment of the forest nearby. Viktoria's father was also prominent in the district's function somehow; an important political figure. That is why the article was composed at all, I imagine.

The family members were comprised of three daughters, his wife and himself. They were trekking to Calw in their open carriage on an ordinary morning. It was a scheduled meeting of the politicos of the day and he asked his family to accompany him. Five rode in that carriage. Wolves attacked, the one horse bolted, the carriage was overturned and one daughter survived. Calw was privy to that simply because that daughter emerged from the rutted road surrounded by Neubulach's best; she came with wounds and clothing sliced and torn.

The surviving daughter was the woman in our picture from Marius's home; that was Viktoria.

And she was sheltered for a while. She never returned to the original family cottage then and abruptly disappeared. The article indicated that she was presumed dead as she was not ever observed again."

Amanda and Valerie simultaneously intoned, "Oh my god!"

"It is Viktoria. Not only that, she must have journeyed to St. Petersburg and that is why no one laid eyes on her ever again.

But she was never dead, just gone."

Chapter 20

SACRED SILVER

"What are you saying then, Jürgen?" Maybe I just do not choose to admit all prospects over my worry for Marius and me. I covet his and my love. And I desperately desire that to remain. I am obliged, though, to discover his genuineness towards me. Oh god help me!"

Suddenly Jürgen ceased in his enthusiastic spiel. Her huge ambivalence was painfully manifested in her words and expressions. Jürgen had meant to comfort her but had inadvertently achieved the opposite. Her sadness cloaked him in heavy sorrow for his role in unraveling the veracity of Marius's and her bond.

Both Valerie and Jürgen extended their arms to Amanda in her grief.

"Manda, your heart is so pristine. Jürgen and I treasure that. Alas, there is a fine line between pristine and guileless! That is the balance being sought here. Neither Jürgen nor I hope for your and Marius's demise. We just believe that love does not demonstrate itself in deceit or secrets and that willful ignorance of the truth would cost you dearly!"

"I love you Val. And so, with no eagerness whatsoever, I ask you again Jürgen, what are you suggesting?"

Jürgen now wrenched his conclusions out to a frightened but courageous Amanda. And Valerie had hold of her hand in addition.

"There is something very disconcerting about what we are learning. How does one live then and now over a span of over one hundred and fifty years? Maybe it involves time travel but that idea seems preposterous to me. All the options here seem ridiculous but this one seems the most ridiculous of all. I will give you all of my worldly belongings if it is so.

No, not that.

So how is she conceivably one hundred and fifty plus years old? That is impossible unless . . ."

Valerie crashed his thoughts. "She could be any of several creatures with long, even eternal, life!"

"That is exactly right! For example, she could be a werewolf. Even more ghastly, she could be a vampire. And both of these demons, were they to actually exist, are capable of transferring their gifts along to those they deem worthy or useful or, as far as I am aware, almost any remote sentiment of their picking."

Please don't think poorly of me here Amanda. You have to believe, in the brief span since we met, that I have come to love your qualities. I pray to never harm you but I have an obligation here to be tough for your sake. That is so that I protect you and your self-interests."

He drew full breath here, unconsciously puffed out his cheeks and exhaled with a sigh. "There is likelihood that she is no longer of the human species. And that she has gifted Marius with the same traits and powers."

"He never touched me violently, Jürgen."

In spite of this protestation, Valerie attempted to drive a further point home. "Or, and I have really nothing to base this on except as a foreboding instinct, he may have gifted her. On second thought, that is a stretch. Ignore that Jürgen, Amanda."

Amanda countered with, "That is easy to do, Val."

Then she straightened her shoulders and lifted her head upright. "I love you both. Your unsought support and loyalty allows my anguish to be less.

But please, fewer crazy speculations, ok?"

Valerie rose. "Jürgen, rest and doze as you are able. I will see to settling Amanda into what I wish will be a soft slumber for her."

Jürgen laid out a final issue. "We go to the mine tomorrow, yes?"

Tiredly, Amanda whispered, "Yes."

Their repose had been unmercifully short and definitely not sweet. That was clear in their departure from Calw much earlier than necessary.

The women had first decided to assist Jürgen in moving forward with his project. There was a small hamlet that their road took them to as they motored to the once sacred silver mine which had been transposed into a sanctuary for asthmatics in the nineteen twenties. This was known because tidbits garnered from the curator had gone beyond the wild chronicle of Viktoria. Jürgen had mentioned his project to him and was rapidly informed of a hamlet named Zaverstein which was famous for its edelweiss and crocus. He believed that Jürgen's flower poses were meant to be taken there. They were perennials he pondered, so the autumn blooms would remain. The curator had also idly speculated that Viktoria's family cottage, though likely long abandoned, was somewhere in the mine's vicinity.

In his fretting over Amanda, Jürgen asked her if her foot was well enough for them to wander fields in search of flowers and poses.

"This venture has taken my mind completely off of my foot. I have not noticed pain or swelling much since meeting up with you Jürgen. You must be a touchstone for me as I have somehow felt on the mend since the airport in Stuttgart. And I suffered both mentally and physically before your offer of aid. And so, I am ready to traipse amongst the lovely buds that you locate for Val and me."

Valerie minced no words when she volunteered, "I am quite excited to contribute to the quality of your coffee table volume. That is the short and tall of it. And that is exactly what you will get when the two of us model for you. Do you desire us topless?" Her eyes twinkled and she grinned broadly.

Exasperated, Amanda said, "Stop it Val. Jürgen's blossoms must come before us."

"That is what I mean. Are we not equally his blossoms? I am just teasing you Jürgen. But spicing up his project would be so much fun."

Jürgen almost panted in his agreement with Valerie. "I wish for buyers to be attracted to the two of you but not fall in love with the pair of you. Or should I say your pairs." Jürgen laughed at what he considered a fine witticism. The women simply rolled their eyes at him.

"Pictures for my own possession would be a lovely prospect though."

The first visible flowers appeared around the last curve.

Chapter 21

MINUS DUST

Amanda and Valerie had never had a close encounter with either an alpine crocus or edelweiss before this day.

According to Jürgen, the most significant piece of the women's photographic play in the meadow was that the edelweiss was protected by German law and was not to be disturbed in any way, shape or form. So be it, Amanda and Valerie voiced in unison.

They proposed, as Jürgen was about to, that they simply lay at the perimeter of the various patches where the buds massed. It was a unanimous proposition and they were all pleased. Amanda curled herself around a bounteous stretch of these principally white blooming beauties. Green tinted the white, a golden center yielding gently to the flaring blossoms and hair covered the surface giving the flower a fuzzy, powdery appearance. Wonderful sight to observe at eye level, Amanda thought. Her impulse was to position her cheek upon her palms and beam into the endless white. And that was just what she did.

Valerie, without prompting, fit herself in behind Amanda and peered over her shoulder at the gorgeous spread of edelweiss. Jürgen arranged and rearranged their clothing before each series of flashes. The gossamer tops, rustic but miniscule shorts that were worn were supplied by Jürgen. He also wanted them in bare feet. He recognized the more chilled low mountain conditions but it was noon and warm. Amanda's hair particularly reset with every mild gust of breeze. Valerie's stunningly intense auburn tones of hair, left unbraided at his request, gave Jürgen great certainty about this portion of his project.

"You might be marveling at the flowers ability to flourish at this altitude and at this proximity to winter. Both the edelweiss here and the crocus which we will shift over to are on show year round. Since they are perennials the only question becomes the time of year that their highlights are the brightest. The autumn highlights are slightly duller than the spring and summer ones but, as you witness, they remain lush and amazingly hued even now.

So, we are done here with the edelweiss. Let's go to the crocus further afield. They can be plucked but we will use the least required flowers for our modeling needs. I hate to meddle with the natural order of flora. That has always been a successful formula for me in these landscape projects of mine."

Time was lessening and so the crocuses and the models together received inferior attention. Yet both were spectacular; Amanda and Valerie's willingness and dramatic good looks along with the crocus's primarily lilac, mauve, and yellow and white hues sent optimism soaring. That each small bundle of these cupped shaped flowers was isolated from one another added to their drama. Valerie placed several lilac and yellow buds against her red hair and behind an ear. Amanda decided to be blatant for once and dropped a tiny bouquet of all colored buds at her upper cleavage. Jürgen had a very fine time positioning and repositioning the individual stems within the bunch. Amanda surveyed him softly and quizzically as he did this.

"Onward playful children," Valerie interjected in the interest of time's departure.

Jürgen had been driving from the beginning. All agreed, as long as he remained alert, that being German and familiar with the countryside, he was the best suited for that endeavor. Amanda kept the passenger seat and Valerie really had no preference.

His concentration was a tad decreased as he snuck views of Amanda and Valerie as they changed from their ultra-thin and skimpy clothing into more sensible attire. They had accomplished this the first time while he had been surveying the meadow for greatest effect. Clever devils, he reflected. The modeling in the meadow had been done without lingerie of any kind. Therefore, as items were removed, in those few instants before sensible became the norm again, Jürgen took full advantage of their striptease.

Amanda and Valerie had both shaved their mons and he observed labia provocatively free. They equally had to shake their petite bottoms back into their tight jeans. They had to work it to complete it. And, of course, they did this realizing their growing impact on him. Their rationale, somewhat caustically, was that teasing rather than diamonds were often a girl's best friend.

He leered over at Amanda and at Valerie in the rearview mirror a final moment before delicate bras were applied. He groaned slightly as nipples hastened from sight.

"Shows over, mister," Valerie flung at him with a major grin offered his direction.

"You, my fine photographer, have seen enough skin for the day," Amanda contributed.

"Damn! Cruelty to the driver will not be tolerated in this vehicle."

Laughter ricocheted off of the windows.

Last evening, Jürgen also gave them a mini-briefing of the mining area they proceeded toward. The town and treatment center's name did not roll off their tongues. Talmuhle-Seitzental was even more forest recessed than was that of the tiny flower capital. The asthmatic center went by the title of Neubulach. The former was a miniscule settlement proximate to the defunct silver mine. And, bizarrely, the treatment center was itself located within the mine. What caused this treatment to be unique for the lung impaired was that the mine created an environment that was minus dust entirely. With fewer agents to irritate lung function, asthmatics responded blissfully.

"Alright ladies, we are going to visit the treatment center. Maybe they have maps or information to lead us to Viktoria's home. Or what is left of it. If we have to bushwhack through heavy forest for the cottage location, we had better purchase a few brush clearing items; maybe miner's hats for light in the woods as well. I have always understood that most any timbered area of the Black Forest is thick and dark with the densely packed fir overhang."

"We may have to take shelter in the car overnight if need be." Valerie was like that, always developing as many options as were reasonable.

Amanda shook her gorgeous head in amazement. "You, Jürgen and you, Val, are beyond fantastic in your willingness to see this through. Were it not for your indisputable and wise assistance, I would have returned to America from the Stuttgart airport readily. I would always wonder about Marius. And it would eat away at me. So, from the bottom of my heart, I give the most profound thanks to you both that I am capable of extending to anyone. I shall repay you someday."

"How do I say this without sounding like a cliché factory? Manda, our actions are because we love you as we know that you love us. You would do the same for us in our moment of tribulation. No quid pro quo here. We want your happiness, period!"

Jürgen was not able to nod his head fast enough to show total agreement with Valerie.

Chapter 22

Poor Boy

"The route that we are taking to Neubulach, the road that we are on now, is labeled the Schwarzwald-Baderstrasse. It is more commonly referred to as the Black Forest Spa Route.

I really enjoy playing guide to your ever wide-eyed accompaniment." Jürgen chortled cheerfully.

"How are you informed of so much pertaining to these valleys and woods? I bet, Jürgen, that you lied to us when you apprised Val and me of the fact that you had never visited here before. I know, you thought to impress us with your wealth of knowledge while pretending to have never set foot in this territory."

Amanda and Valerie snickered together gently.

"Not so my doubting travel companions." At that, Jürgen wiggled his rear and removed an undersized pocket guide from the back pocket of his jeans.

"I come well prepared. It even reports that there are churches, monasteries, castles, fortresses, high moor-bogs, I memorized that just for you both, in the vicinity. Alas though, we have prior engagements to fulfill and so will have to refuse the splendor offered in order to reach the mine and treatment center before dark. Driving is treacherous enough in light of day at these elevations and on these winding roads but is death defying at night.

And, to add to your listening pleasure, there is no necessity to make encampment in the vehicle overnight. This morning, I examined my fine little book once again and specifically for Neubulach. It is more than an old mine and treatment center. It has that tiny town close by, Talmuhle-Seitzental, which, miraculously, has lodging. More so, I phoned them and established reservations.

I do so love taking care of you and Valerie. I want no more suspicion towards me now or I will allow you to fend for yourselves. Take that my beauties!"

Amanda and Valerie were speechless for but a flash. "We will never let you get away with that you poor boy. You are firmly and irrevocably stuck with us!"

In turn, Valerie enjoined, "You are stuck with us until your last dying day my friend. And if you handle us well, we may even do your bidding on occasion."

Contentment and affectionate regard settled over the three so effortlessly.

Darkness was trimming the day away in lowering swaths as their auto discovered the village and their accommodations.

Sheer exhaustion struck Valerie first and foremost amongst them as Jürgen and Amanda sipped on delightfully steaming tea. Valerie fell unceremoniously into the one-size-fits-barely-a-body bed. Jürgen shuffled through the latter portion of his guidebook. Amanda contemplated her shifting feelings. She resisted any shifting vigorously. Inevitably, those feelings were transforming and picking up speed and those transformations boded poorly for her and Marius.

First, he had not rung her since her practice demise and painful injury. How sadly weird was that, she considered? Of course, she had not either since her embarkation on this investigation of his veracity. She had deemed it unwise to maintain contact with him. If they were to part, that was an ordeal in and of itself, made more difficult with the ties that continuous tight contact brought. She preferred their distance physically as well. The geographic distance muted the agony some.

She was determined to be objective to her utmost no matter how it might claw through her heart. She had to be absolutely certain of Marius; and, of that, she was no longer.

Second, there was a disturbing impulse that was mounting inside her that bewildered her to a degree; to a degree she understood the security of it. Proximity, with a decided pull, was a factor in this new attraction. Her fondness for Jürgen was riding a rising tide inside of her that had no fall; a wall of liquid emotion was threatening to drown her old ties if she permitted it.

He was across the table and within her reach. Valerie was in deep slumber and, had she been awake, with the fact of

Jeffrey at home, would more than likely have said 'once and enough for me, you feel free.' She might have reminded Amanda equally that Valerie and Jürgen's prior coupling should impact Amanda only slightly as there had been no commitment then between Amanda and Jürgen. It was Amanda's old fashioned sense that even caused her thoughts to traipse there. Jürgen had been a free agent then and he still was a free agent. Was she? That was the truer question.

In spite of this attempt at logic, Amanda's sentiments were not to be quelled.

When Jürgen had naughtily fiddled with her strategically tucked away bouquet of crocuses, she had unexpectedly craved that he touch her there. Her nipples had had these anticipatory electric sensations and had lengthened considerably at his nearness. Her arousal for him in the meadow had startled and disconcerted her.

And definitely, changing from the modeled tops and shorts into her more usual garb kindled her energy. She had enjoyed exhibiting herself to him immensely.

Her impulse wickedly grew at the table until she was no longer able to restrain herself. She leaned his direction, took a hand of his and placed it upon her hidden covered nipple and lifted his chin with the other hand.

He deftly stroked his thumb at her already thick and tense tip. The contact, even through the thin cotton, was charged. His eyes met hers and their gaze was mutual and hot.

Amanda did not choose to ruin anything developing between them though. She also had to deal with Marius before all else.

She lightly removed his hand from her breast.

He acceded to her wishes as he knew her dilemma.

Chapter 23
TWO COTTAGES

The anticipation was that they establish the whereabouts of Viktoria's family home, hopefully hike to it, glean all available clues there and ultimately decide whether to further pursue Marius's history with Viktoria if nothing significant were exposed by their efforts. And they all were desperate to accomplish this before October daylight abandoned them. Valerie continued adamant about a full scouring of the age-old property which the silver miner's family's had dwelt upon, Amanda remained ambivalent yet primed to grab at the truth in spite of its illusiveness and Jürgen was satisfied being in their company with an adventure to chase.

So they went ahead and devised a plan that served all purposes. It was not a particularly complex plan either. It entailed reaching the neighboring conjoined defunct mine and treatment center. They anticipated buying tickets to the mine's tour facility, bypassing the treatment center and purchasing a map of the mine's perimeter and trail clearing equipment at the always reliable gift stores that invariably beckoned to the ubiquitous gawker. They were ready to chat up the cashier for offhand, conceivably helpful information too.

Her summation was concluded. Valerie was essentially the solitary awake individual of the three of them. It was actually her stratagem and she was poised to rouse them and astound them with the smartness of it.

But did she always have to be the first to arise? And be the brute who told them that matters of the day pressed and demanded abrupt attention? She seemed to be the early morning taskmaster. And she was good at it.

No shock then that Valerie's efficiency brought Jürgen early to Neubulach's parking area and they hustled out to purchase admission to what was a partially timbered structure; meticulously scrubbed and inviting. It was larger than what they had seen previously in Calw but did not vary in style. Valerie was confident that there had been a blueprint given to builders in the Black Forest with the demand that this singular design, scale of any dimension permitted, be implemented. Yet they really were superb and appealing.

Once inside, the three had no intent of wasting valuable minutes on the tour to and through the mine's core. They were intent upon following Valerie's instructions without deviation. The tourist shops were the target and mining supplies and information of the surrounds was the object. As anticipated by Valerie, a small shop of miner's items was clearly set on all tourists' path to the start of the tour.

Valerie stepped into the shop entrance with Amanda and Jürgen at her heels. Miner's helmets were on bold display. Valerie put three under her arms and checked for batteries. The helmets came equipped with enough to power the beam that each threw forward. One set of items was now obtained, Valerie took note of.

Out of Valerie's peripheral view, she observed emergency packs. Amanda was headed there.

"Val, these have a first aid kit, canteen, small folding shovel, a compact knife with a few attachments, matches in an airtight canister. That should be all that we need if we are forced to clear trails or if trouble arises. One seems adequate, correct?"

"I would say that one is just fine. It may even be more than we need. But let's err on the safe side of the equation."

"Amanda, Valerie, here is a geologic map of the territory outside the mine; very detailed. It even marks a trail to two isolated cottages. It is really quite marvelous in the specifics labeled. It mentions that one of the surviving cottages was likely the master quarters for the lead miner. I imagine that we can assume that is the cottage of Viktoria's family. He seemed to be the man for the time and the region. It says nothing of the distant other cottage. This map is a miraculous find. Luck has been our ally from the beginning; plus some smarts too, of course.

I want to ask the salesperson a question or two before we depart."

"There is no reason not to if it aids us and quickens the outcome, Jürgen." As Amanda leaned in to Jürgen to say this, Valerie recognized a relaxation and familiarity to Amanda's mien towards Jürgen. It pleased Valerie greatly if her friend was gradually uncovering securer emotional ground. Fair or not, Valerie quietly rooted for an Amanda-Jürgen connection as opposed to an Amanda-Marius connection. She just instinctively did not trust Marius. Jürgen impacted her one hundred and eighty degrees differently. Jürgen had a kind transparency to his actions that translated to his being a genuinely trustworthy soul. She detected and parsed this in but an instant. But she was profoundly sure of it.

Jürgen approached the register and deposited the map onto the surface. Amanda did likewise with the kit and Valerie stacked the boxed helmets atop one another.

"May I ask, are these indicated trails well maintained?"

The smiling woman informed him, "They were scrupulously cleared and restored as needed for many years. The remains of one cottage is considered historic, a relic of a period when silver was brought up from the mine.

Sadly, there have been much reduced funds for performing this task. Volunteers have not been plentiful. The trail may be rather rough by now. I have never hiked it so I am just guessing. But logic says my guess is a well-educated one."

"What do you figure about the trails veering to the second cottage?"

"I have been told that was of historic importance. The supposition is that it was a common woodcutter's home. What creates its importance is no more than that a bit of its foundation can still be viewed. Otherwise, it was not notable."

Lest they get betrayed by the high noon sun later, they departed the shop and the mine in haste.

Access to the cottages was within reach in short order.

Jürgen goosed the car and left a trace of rubber and sound.

Valerie presumed that was his adrenaline building. It was stimulating to be proximate to this mysterious woman's actual abode.

Chapter 24

Humiliation Undeserved

As he ravished her body, hammered himself into her, his anger took him to memories of autocratic rule and undeserved humiliation. The sentiment engendered insisted that he leave his fury inside of her. She writhed and twisted under his harsh, sometimes brutal, strokes.

He knew that she was his to take. He did not love this woman as he did Amanda and Viktoria. But she was ample in attitude. She craved his rough and unbridled strength with her he felt. She moaned and shook and then groaned lasciviously as he pumped her. She goaded him to do more, to loosen her senses and do his full and complete desire upon her. She also knew not what she said during their volcanic exchange and that was why he did not yield to the final command of the ultimate monster in himself.

This was Amanda's second and she had to be at her finest for the soon to happen Giselle's opening. No other outcome was to be tolerated. So he eased in spite of her pleas that he plunder her flesh beyond the enduring.

In repose, upon the same hulking chair that he and Amanda had heated the other vastly, Rebecca offered Marius an opportunity for venting and explication.

"You almost shred me, you do me so intensively. What drives that, Marius? There is a very powerful quality to it. But it is hardly under your control. Answer me if you would."

"The furnace for my heat, my wrath, is twofold."

One regards my father and the iron fist that he wielded over me in my formative years. I hated him for that. I was just seven years old when he insisted that I was to be a danseur and that I must eventually command all aspects of that profession. This included ballet and its intricate moves, of course. Beyond that though, he taught me nuances of voice and song, the subtle craft of makeup for myself and others, the difficult practice of writing and the primacy of injecting oneself into the sensibility of the character acted. He even went so far as to teach me means to construct stages, props, scene design. And the teaching of this profession was a fait accompli by my ripe old age of twelve.

He badgered me, he smacked me, he slapped me and he roared at me if I did not ascend to his expectations at all times.

And heaven forbid that I might choose an altogether separate occupation than what his grand design for me included. I tried that once, and only once, when I was eight and only a year into my lessons. I was sick of the intensity and demands. In my child's voice, I informed him that I would not take another dance step for him again, ever.

He raged for days. He attempted to lock me away with hardly any sustenance. He whipped me. I was beaten dually; he beat me into dancing again, and he beat me into submitting to him from then on. But he never could put out the simmering resentment that I held in my gut. It, as you have experienced moments ago, burns lividly in my sexuality, in my own unrelenting expectations and to my spiritual center.

He took me to America; dragged me is more like it! I resisted accompanying him anywhere. Ironically though, I enjoyed this country. Naturally, he was cognizant of that and so forcibly returned me to lovely Paris. It is lovely but not under those conditions.

It was not until he was fifty-five years of age that he died and I finally had my way and suffered his influence no more. That was while I was in Russia and then I planted myself here in Seattle permanently."

"You mentioned another fuel for your smoldering energy. What was that?"

"You are bold. Yet that is what gives you the qualities to render Giselle brilliantly."

"Anyway, that one is fresher, more painful therefore. When I performed in the Russian theater, I transformed it, I believe, in my limited years there. You may think my estimation immodest but it is not."

"I am not one to judge as I am only aware of the barest rudiments of Russian theater. And besides, you are such an awesome choreographer and danseur. Why would I ever question your prowess and abilities anywhere?

You certainly must be fluent in many languages too. You are rather amazing."

He had realized these words of hers before he had revealed himself to her. Otherwise, none of this would ever have spilled out of his mouth. It would have been disaster if she had an inkling of who Marius Petipa was. Ultimately, it would have been disaster for her as he would have finished her immediately in spite of Giselle.

"Anyway, I put together a very special ballet while at what turned out to be the end of my tenure in Russia. It was one that I actually wrote; spent a year on it. It honestly squashed me initially when reviews were somewhat unwarranted and of more importance, audiences, even stalwart fans, thinned and then deserted me. My theater company blamed me for what they considered a failed affair. That was the instant that my sense of insult and evolving rage were generated.

"You see my darling Rebecca, I had served my time, a new owner swaggered in and that ownership wanted my exit. Pronto. They were very clever in their method of severing me from the theater I loved. Bosses and audiences alike joined in criticizing miniscule aspects of the ballet. It was outrageous.

I was not to blame! They were! They sought my blood. They got it too. I should have taken theirs. And I could have. But instead, I came to the States.

I am not nimble when it comes to revenge. My heart often betrays me and I am unwilling in my sensitivities to exchange vicious behavior with further vicious behavior.

The Puget Sound attracted me sharply. The existence of the multiple islands within that waterway is distinct. I can retreat to a different one on each visit. They are so isolated and tranquil. I can blend with the surroundings and feel a connection with the few other beings there."

Rebecca snored mildly. Marius was not perturbed as the wine and passion had been a heavy mix. But it did permit him to take his leave momentarily.

Chapter 25

Gorgeous Dames

Amanda tilted her head, falsely widened her eyes, playfully employed fingertips of flattened hand to her pursed lips and murmured, "Oh my; and how uncharacteristic of her too."

She did this as Valerie mugged in the back seat. Valerie had removed a helmet from its packaging and plopped it over her braided locks. After that, she unzipped her hoodie and spread it wide apart. She jerked her thick top up and bared her bra covered chest. The demi design hid her nipples but half of each aureole was revealed. "Put me in any miner's calendar please. That is your next project Jürgen. To hell with quality. Just make those sales. Manda and I would sell those cheesy calendars as if they were hotcakes with plenty of butter and syrup dripping."

Amanda guffawed and then yelped, "I can do that too! Pass me one of those helmets, Val."

Amanda did Valerie one better after she flipped the helmet onto her abundant blond tresses. She promptly grabbed over her waistline and tugged all layers to her chin, bra included.

"Damn girl, you look ever so hot."

"I realize that I do. Hot mamas, you and me." Giggling poured out from the women.

"The both of you behave! Much as I desire molding you gorgeous dames to my heaving frame this instant, finding the trail as soon as achievable is critical. We do not comprehend precisely what we are up against in our pursuit of Viktoria and Marius. If what I suppose is accurate becomes truth, each passing minute increases the danger to us. This definitely may be about much more than Marius's fidelity to you, Amanda.

The trail head might very well be overgrown and not simple to locate."

But Jürgen grinned then. "Stop your shenanigans here and now or my erection will block my vision and I will most assuredly miss not only the trail but will crash the car."

All were amused yet his very serious words sank in. Amanda and Valerie sobered abruptly and reworked their clothing but Valery was unable to restrain herself from letting "yes, boss," slip out nonetheless.

"You are correct Jürgen. And thank you for not scolding us severely. This is an endeavor with much concern involved. Val and I will apply ourselves diligently to the task again."

Valerie added, "We apologize. The investigation has such eerie and demoralizing implications. And they are growing. A little levity and distraction seems critical to tone the implications down. The timing was really poor. Ouch."

"I loved it though. So no sadness. Focus and we will find definitive answers soon I hope."

Old growth fir had transitioned quickly into dense barriers along the two lane concrete ribbon that wound from Neubulach. Amanda and Valerie had restored order to their clothes when Jürgen extended his arm and pointed to a heavy chain linked between two stumps at the roadside. There was a fractional clearing there, nothing else. Jürgen positioned the auto as best as he could.

Amanda plucked the freshly purchased map from the cluttered dashboard and laid it in her lap for all to see. Once unfolded, Jürgen twisted in his seat, Amanda presumed, to insure that they had not overshot or simply strayed from its markings.

Amanda spoke as Valerie peered over the backseat and attempted to sort out the map's bearings along with the others. "It appears as if this may be the necessary trail head. The map indicates that it should be neighboring the mine."

Valerie kicked in, "That is the logical assumption. Miner's would not voluntarily choose to live a distance from their source of work."

Jürgen continued to study coordinates. He muttered, "hmmm," withdrew from the vehicle and strode to the metal links. He nosed into the low lying brush, disappeared from sight momentarily and returned nodding his head in the affirmative to himself.

"This is the appropriate trail. It is not particularly apparent from the road however. But there is a smallish, tipped and somewhat rotting signpost amongst the overgrowth. All that is scratched into it is 'Master Cottage.' It is not exactly your well announced tourist site but it fits faultlessly with her description of the fall off of caretaking here the last several years."

Amanda and Valarie had already applied their helmets, not haphazardly this time, and gave Jürgen his. They tested the helmet beams and all three functioned satisfactorily.

They had filled the canteen prior to leaving the comfortable Neubulach gates. Amanda double checked the kit items and presented it to Jürgen.

"Splendid. I will do the honors of hefting the kit. I can carry the map also. Let's eat a portion of our grapes, cheese, chocolate and nuts before we begin."

Once their mini-repast was consumed, they locked all doors and treaded to the limbs at the trail edge and its entryway. Jürgen took the lead, Amanda second and Valerie third.

The forest canopy hung brutally thick upon them as soon as they had paced several steps in. Though it was approximately noontime with clear skies above, they experienced unrelenting shade and a definite descent of temperature. The trail gradient was downward sloping and Amanda bore an impression that they had entered a dark hole only getting more so.

"It is not as damp as the Olympics; the rainforest there," commented Amanda.

Valerie shivered. "It is more claustrophobic though. Maybe I am somewhat spooked but this feels narrow, confining and decidedly unpleasant. I can understand this area being the origin of many frightening fairy tales."

Jürgen was not overhearing them; maybe not listening in his concentration. The intrusive branches were a major impediment and the path was occasionally distinct at its best and nonexistent at its worst. He lit the map with the helmet's bright light. "This has to be right."

Chapter 26

Bottoms Up

Jürgen ploddingly deciphered clues to the trail direction until the junction was reached. The kit, inexplicably, did not contain a compass and they had forgotten its importance until now.

He had relied solely on information from the map. And the map was a godsend but was, nonetheless, only so detailed. So there was essentially no more guidance from that source after this particular determination. Both trail offshoots reduced distance from the mine, one less so than the other. The left angled turn ran parallel to the abandoned shaft and plunged deeply into the timber while the right angled turn ran parallel also but then mildly curved inward nearing Neubulach somewhat. It was clear to him that the latter trail was the reasonable trail to take.

Amanda and Valerie chattered about a rainforest proximate to Seattle. He sensed that their dialogue was more an act to distract themselves in an attempted effort to diminish their fear.

The map told him that the path straightforward took them severely into the wooded recesses. The trail he now chose led to what appeared to be an infinitesimal thinning of fir and consequent lightening overhead. Even if he was wrong here, and he suspected he was not, the heightened light in that direction cheered him.

"Amanda, Valerie, we take the very slightly veering path to the right. Do you agree?"

Amanda seemed frightened. Valerie less frightened but definitely anxious and would continue to rely on Jürgen.

"It is absolutely your call Jürgen," Valerie replied.

Amanda tremulously whispered, "I fully agree with Val. We defer to your decision.

I am even uncertain as to whether we should continue here. I love Marius. But I do not wish to bet my life on it. And this investigation is becoming more perilous by the moment and much more than I anticipated it would be. Say we were to discover Marius and Viktoria are saints, and that is hardly likely anymore, I would rather not be found dead at the depths of some unforeseen sheer ravine. And worse, if harm came to either of you two due to satisfying my needs, I would be crushed . . . forever."

Jürgen reassured her firmly. "We will not get lost. We will not fall. We will not come to harm. We will not fail. We will find the cottage. We will be back with the auto by nightfall.

If there is jeopardy, we are already threatened. So I say we make a final effort here and retreat totally if nothing is uncovered at the cottage site. Of course, that is Amanda's decision to arrive at depending upon her level of love for Marius."

"That love of mine for him is, sadly, darkening by the minute."

Jürgen and Valerie both let this statement sink in.

"So no more time is used, let's move on." Valerie was firm and impatient.

"Yes Jürgen, you and Val are correct. Let's move on." Amanda seemed to have recaptured her assurance for the moment.

They, at long last, came upon a partial clearing at path's end where, submerged somewhat beneath a fragile webbing of overgrowth, was what must have been the cottage's foundation. Finished rock, peppered with the remnants and shards of formerly solid wood, formed a visible rectangle as seen through the tangled overlay.

They comprehended that this was the building they sought, Viktoria's abode. But would it yield up anything of significance; push them forward or send them home? As their eyes followed the rectangle of what he deemed to have been a warm delight for Viktoria years ago, none of them observed any helpful details.

There was, upon repeated and intensified inspection, an odd depression observed within the earth of that rectangle. It dawned on Jürgen that it was as if ground gave way, caved in partially to an object. He hoped that was the case anyway. What, really, was there to lose in the attempt?

"What do you have in mind Jürgen?" His pause had caught Amanda's attention.

"Do you see that small sinkhole there; like a minute cave-in of sorts?"

Amanda and Valerie grabbed for the kit off of his back in unison. Valerie unstrapped the shovel from the rest of the kit. She then snapped its folds into a compact and usable tool and dropped it into Jürgen's proffered hand. He carefully chopped at the interwoven brush above so as to avoid destroying anything meaningful to them.

He broke through the natural barrier and dug into the earth's concavity. The women bent over his shoulder as, on bended knees, Jürgen maintained a careful but insistent and steady pace. Having unearthed four or five feet of the modestly damp soil, the point of his shovel clanked.

Jürgen jerked the tool aside and began using his fingers. The earth was soft enough and suddenly Jürgen flushed with accomplishment.

"Bottoms up all! I have what looks to be the base of a bottle. Its color is brownish. I will collect it and show you."

He loosened the muddy clay from around the glass circumference and, as he did this, wiggled the glass object back and forth, over and over.

The women held their breath.

There was a sucking sound as Jürgen released the bottle from Mother Earth's brown clutches. It was a wine bottle, no label or identification at all, cork jammed in and held tightly by the bottle's neck still. The protruding exposed cork surface was damaged but, otherwise, remained intact.

Jürgen took the canteen, a bunch of Kleenex from the kit and wiped the bottle clear.

There was a rounded sheath of paper inside.

Chapter 27

SHADOW NIPPLE

"I insist that whatever this bottle informs us of, the pursuit ends with that. These woods terrify me. Nothing merits any of us being hurt. And I have a ballet to return to. I will more than likely stand in the wings throughout but that is satisfactory.

"My nerves are on their very edge. Wise decision Manda." Valerie rarely reflected capitulation but she had no further truck with the Black Forest than Amanda did.

"Back we go then. Amanda, Valerie, are you certain that we should not go find a bud or two and take photographs?"

"That is not funny, Jürgen. Usually I enjoy both the timing and quality of your quips but not this one." Amanda turned Jürgen up trail and smacked his butt hard.

"Go Jürgen. And do not look back unless I say so!"

Valerie silently applauded Amanda's words.

Jürgen held the bottle tightly and surged forward, retracing their steps back to their rental. Dusk was beginning to set. They all whooped and threw their equipment and then themselves through the doors and into the auto. Jürgen was slightly gentler with the bottle but hardly so. He did not heave it; he simply wedged it between the front seats. He was to be its protector until they were secure in their still reserved room. Amanda and Valerie scarcely glanced the bottle's way. They were quietly frantic to get off the road and lock their hotel's door behind them before shadows turned to black. They had suffered black plenty throughout the day. The venture spooked them very much in spite of an uneventful exit from the forest's maw.

They gracelessly collapsed onto chairs and the bed after shutting, bolting and draping over the single window in the hotel's room. If they had possessed two by fours, they would have nailed the lumber to the frame so as to impede any attempted entry. Sprigs of garlic and traditional crosses were on their mind too.

"I am exhausted. Please Jürgen, put the bottle aside for tonight. I desire a one evening moratorium from the stress of what has evolved into almost more than I can bear!"

A huge sigh whistled from Valerie. "I second that."

Valerie was already on the bed, picked at the combined sheet and down comforter corner, sheered it open and, entirely clothed, threw the bedding over her. Earlier she had had the foresight to shed her shoes. Shoeless only, she dove into a dramatic sleep.

Amanda suffered a temporary paralysis due to her fatigue and that constant buzz and press of intense emotions. Too much was occurring too rapidly.

Jürgen found his traditional location without further ado. He stood mechanically from his chair, spun agilely and flopped stiffly onto the couch face first. He rolled, sheets twisting with him, and closed his eyes face up.

Amanda watched what she considered to be a wholly endearing routine. She was much less determined to confront Marius at any time since she now recognized her affections bleeding from Marius to Jürgen. And affection for Jürgen it was not. That term indicated denial on her part. She was fully smitten with this man that she had just met several days ago.

Her senses kept redirecting her emotions to Jürgen in spite of her forced efforts at leaving those emotions with Marius. Her heart was in rebellion and not obeying her commands. The unruliness of her heart surprised her but would not be stilled.

She submitted. She had no enduring energy or capacity remaining to resist her swollen impulses. She went to him where he slumbered, and kissed him hotly on the lips. "Awaken Jürgen. Touch me where you touched me before, where I led your hand."

Jürgen's lashes separated, his eyes shone vividly, his warm breath imparted itself upon her lustrous skin, her cleavage. He saw her breast and reached for it. He gently, backhandedly caressed her shadow nipple that was growing less shadow and more nipple through her top by the second. She leaned over him so that he witnessed an unending line between unending pendulous breasts.

His hand swiveled so that his fingertips dipped beneath her top and sought direct contact with that nipple.

Her erotic engines were unleashed as her threshold for restraint had been breached. She allowed her passion for him to cascade in abundant and marvelous waves that crashed upon and then over his grander expectations. She was to fill herself with him and give way to all prior resistance. She sought his honest spirit in her actions. It was an idyllic sensation. But she lusted after him too now; the primal and sublime mixed. She became frenzied to have his being yearn for her alone.

She let him, after brief play on his part, harshly remove all material barriers of hers from waist up. He was so hungry for her that after wrestling with her bra clasps for a moment, he ripped them apart without an afterthought. That bra would never be wearable again.

She smothered his face with her wide and glorious mounds. He sucked one after another nipple wildly. She straddled him and ground into his bulge. She had to touch him there instantly; and not through his jeans. She ceased her movements, lifted her hips and dragged his zipper down. He unbuckled his belt with sure hands, brought his hips upward and she and he quickly tugged his jeans off. Before he removed those jeans completely, Amanda fell upon his rearing column. She mouthed its broad girth and ratcheted up and down on his outsize length.

He laid his hands on her hair delicately as she fisted, then pumped his shaft all the while lashing her tongue over his flaring mushroom capped cockhead. He guided her with a fragile touch but did not need to guide her at all.

"I cannot hold myself back if you do not stop. You have to stop my beauty. I crave entering you. Let me. Oh god, yes, let me!"

Amanda did as she had to in removing her pants and sat upon him then. He split her nether lips flawlessly. She took him to his root. He expanded inside of her as they ferociously jolted against one another.

Amanda's entire interior expanded and then explosively contracted in a series of exquisitely pleasurable spasms. She moaned repeatedly with body upright and head poised in a surfeit of wonder.

Jürgen, when his outsize staff was so subtly squeezed by her orgasmic current, jerked upward, torso only. His cock threw hurling streams of come into her then. More waves seized her and he blew more of his seed into her.

She put her palms on his muscular chest and urged him to a lying position. He complied in a smooth movement returning to the flat of the couch.

Chapter 28

LEAFING THROUGH

The bottle was tightly wrapped within the plush towel. Jürgen had smacked it with force multiple times over the tub's porcelain edge. The thick glass had thudded but no more. He had devised this method as a neat and orderly way to reach the curled sheath inside the bottle.

He had already pulverized the cork in hopes of fingering the sheets out one by one. That was not going to happen. Neither he, Amanda nor Valerie were capable of touching a sheet let alone sliding any out. Busting the heavy glass became their sole option.

Valerie tapped his shoulder and reminded him, "There is a rockery in front of the building. Crack it there. I would be very surprised if it did not shatter then."

In no more than five minutes, Jürgen returned with a towel full of shards and pieces of the brown glass. He held the thin round of paper deftly.

It was late morning and they had paid for another twenty four hours of shelter here. The occasion for determining the value of their reconnaissance was imminent.

The sheets were tolerably preserved. Some of the ink had spread outward to other words and sentences. All witnessed the very cramped script crowded tightly on the parchment.

"Is that readable?" Amanda asked.

"It is. But it is as if written by an illiterate, someone hardly tutored in the art of diction, spelling and the printed word. Scanning quickly, the author seems to consider himself somewhat of a philosopher and broad thinker." Jürgen continued his perusal.

Amanda caught Valerie's eye and shook her head slightly side to side. "There is not a prospect in hell that I could have overcome the hurdle that the language would have presented to me everywhere. I might have managed a fraction slowly but even that is giving me more credit than I deserve. And Val, I know that your stubborn perseverance would have gotten us a bit further a bit faster. But truly, the burden in our hunt has been carried by Jürgen.

He is amazing."

Valerie affirmed, "That he is."

Jürgen looked up briefly, smiled broadly and warmly pronounced, "I relish assisting such sweet and wondrous individuals as you two. And we will solve this." He brought his gaze back to the pages.

Valerie pushed a notepad and a pen to him. He fingered the pen and began jotting items onto the pad. He did not slow for nearly an hour as he leafed through it all.

"This is phenomenal, though I cannot decipher a lot of this. The letters and words run together often, there is smearing and this person is not particularly competent as I mentioned before. Here is what I have gathered and, though it is not absolute proof of any of our theories, it goes a huge distance in sealing gaps in our knowledge.

This appears to be a collection of love notes, reminiscences, primitive philosophizing and, yes, renditions of portions of Viktoria's life as Viktoria conveyed those events to him. If I am correct, the writer, this Vincent, and Viktoria had to use this written form of communication because they were both demons!

He reveals that Viktoria was transformed into a vampire. It is nearly impossible to believe but, as I figure it, she slept in the daylight and he was in human incarnation only during the daylight. He was something else at night. And it was beastly and not intelligent then; brutish but in love with Viktoria though she was a vampire. Seemingly, she informed him of aspects of her life when he was this other being and then he rushed to pen her words when rational and human. And he wrote other than simply her story. Much of it was his mooning about his love for her. At the end of his telling, he mentions that he left his notations in a bottle kept at her coffin's side."

"This cannot be, Jürgen. This has to be fabrication. It is the ramblings of someone delusional and beyond help!" Amanda cried.

Valerie clasped her friend and shuddered. "This is nauseating if at all true. And it is more than frightening. Our very lives might be at stake."

"We cannot stay!" Amanda was frantic.

Jürgen peered directly at the meshed women. "I believe that we are actually more in peril the nearer we are to Marius. Bear with me, let me finish and then we will decide."

Amanda and Valerie only broke their embrace slowly as they sank down to the two other chairs around the table where Jürgen sat.

"Here is what is penned about Viktoria upon her abrupt departure after her family was destroyed.

According to her, as she tells Vincent, she is a headstrong young woman, lithe and strong. She also is unafraid when confronted with disaster. And, the day of her family's demise, her calm saves her. She scrambles for her father's whip when the carriage tumbles. She attempts to keep the wolves from her unconscious family members as best she can with the whip. The wolves are hungry and gorge themselves. Viktoria realizes the hopelessness for her parents and sisters and desperately departs the scene.

The wolves are fully sated. One though pursues Viktoria. On a single wolf, the whip succeeds. That wolf withdraws as it is whip-flicked repeatedly; its belly is full and the pain of the flailing girl's instrument overcomes the primal instinct to attack.

Viktoria survives and is taken to Calw from Neubulach to the preacher's abode. It is there that she is given shelter and is restored."

Chapter 29

Petipa's Pupil

"Viktoria, again in her estimation as she relays it to Vincent, is quite the imaginative and resourceful young woman. A small traveling clique of actors has come to the mining town, Neubulach, once and she is captivated. She has dreamed of journeying with a troupe of performers since. She is impatient to set her life in motion and that life is not meant for digging in the ground or following the dutiful style of the pastor's wife.

She fixes her sights on a metropolis, does not wait for the next brigade of sojourning entertainers and quits the area on a day like any other; she does not doubt her future success separate from the mine, Calw and the Black Forest."

"Please hurry Jürgen. Spare us the lesser details. Whatever her life's facts, I am feeling very troubled in and around Neubulach. Just the name disturbs me!"

"I will hurry Amanda. Many of the details are obscured, as I already mentioned, anyhow. I will tone down my habit of dramatizing as well. But this is astonishing stuff!"

He continued with a pace to match Amanda's very legitimate concerns. To her, this search had sprung past a simple question of fidelity and love to a question of menace and physical hazard.

"She wends her way, albeit slowly, over what seems to approximate to a year's time, to Russia; and then to St. Petersburg. See, that is where the watermark on the photograph comes into play. I had no real idea of its significance until now. The picture is obviously taken in St. Petersburg!"

"Tell us then, if you can sort out the nuances, what is the significance of this particular city to her?" Valerie, though anxious, was less so than Amanda and was truly fascinated by Viktoria's tale.

"Viktoria, apparently, has asked around regarding the prime location to learn the trade of the performer. She is repeatedly informed, even in close at hand territory, of the superior qualities of the Imperial Theater in that Russian city. She uses all of her strength, her wiles, takes several very menial jobs and effectively arrives in St. Petersburg. She must have developed rudimentary knowledge of the Russian language in her progress to there.

Brazen individual that she is, she marches directly to the royal institute, the Imperial Theater, and seeks out the chief choreographer without hesitation. She flaunts her beauty, I suppose, and persuades all to yield to her demands even while speaking the language poorly. One of those very persons susceptible to her magnetism includes the maestro himself, Marius Petipa.

Vincent bases his description of this exceptional director of stage craft purely on Viktoria's utterance's as he claims to have never met Petipa; has never even heard of him until Viktoria spills her history to him."

"Alright, their first names match. That is still not absolute proof that he is the present day Marius." Amanda resisted the potential blackness of Marius in spite of her newfound love for Jürgen. Her love for Marius had been leached from her but she still desired to perceive him as a good man. She was reluctant to release that notion of him as her prior fervent sense of him held on.

"Wait, there is more, much more. Viktoria apprentices with this Petipa individual and becomes his sole pupil. Guessing again, she has to have memorized the Russian dialogue in the ballets as she remains without fluency.

By the by, have either of you ever heard of him?"

He was not surprised as Valerie shook her head in the negative; why would a payroll manager have knowledge of what seemed to be a legendary balletic director.

Amanda was stunned as she remembered this name. But why did she remember it? Jürgen and Valerie stared at her and waited for Amanda's pause to end. "Yes, I do recollect that name! Marius had a volume in his library that he continually read and reread. It exclusively detailed this man's accomplishments from birth to a supposed retirement! And my Marius was fascinated by it. That was because it was about himself. This is surreal! I never opened it though and really know nothing of this dance luminary."

"Scary information, that!

And according to Viktoria and her cipher, Marius Petipa has, virtually without assistance, affected European ballet but has most prominently revitalized Russian ballet; that according to a somewhat immodest Viktoria. He is a genius and with his outsize skills, he teaches Viktoria to become one of the finest prima ballerinas. She has evinced the motivation to him, has demonstrated her physical aptitudes and has finally captured his heart too. She is a heady beauty in addition as we can all testify to from the photograph. Vincent depicts her shape in a paragraph. It would seem by his descriptive excesses that her curves quite nicely complement her face.

Petipa, no shock then, lusts after her and the two explore one another intimately. The bond strengthens, deepens in their concentrated practice together. Viktoria pours her feelings out to Vincent regarding her pure and enduring love for Petipa. She seems to give herself over to Petipa entirely; abandoning restraint or caution.

It goes on in this vein for an extended period of time. They are enamored of one another as if fused. Vincent seems not to mind and is in Viktoria's thrall as her later lover and ambitious scribe."

"Jürgen, for god's sake, get to it please!"

"My love, here is the rest . . . . and quickly!" He did not wish to agitate Amanda into higher pitches. And now, loving her, he desired her wellbeing always.

"One more aside, I beg of you my sweet Amanda. Without this, a huge puzzle piece is lost. It is also nothing more than my detective skills rendered for us."

Amanda yielded by giving Jürgen a quick peck on the cheek.

"The inscription must have been written in German, and I say that very loosely as Germany then was only a ragtag collection of states and not even a country, because Viktoria is incapable of writing in Russian. Marius, I am betting, is the faster learner of languages as he is already fluent in French, Spanish, English and Russian; so why not German as well? Therefore, he becomes adept at reading her writing as opposed to her reading his. Thus the inscription is expressed in German by Viktoria for Marius to decipher.

I see subtle strangeness in her expression in the inscription and so it must be written in the syntax of the state that she dwelt in at the time, Baden-Württemberg. I should have detected that earlier. What an idiot! This reveals that the inscription was written long ago. We have further demonstration besides the neckline clothing that, when compared to the quality of the photograph, she must have lived then and now!

Jürgen, in his excitement, could not help himself from elaborating just a bit further before commencing with the core of Vincent's telling. "What a talented guy this Marius is to have mastered such a local dialect in such a brief span!"

"Enough. Back to other than my conjecture.

So then a calamitous event occurs on an eve following a performance by Viktoria of one of Petipa's ballets. Viktoria weeps as she informs Vincent of the happening and he cannot capture the incident quite or make sense of it. The single fact that Vincent manages here is that Viktoria was never the same again; that her trust in Petipa is shattered.

It is Vincent's guess that Petipa is vampire and Viktoria, unwillingly, becomes the same. Vincent knows that she is vampire, he just is unsure of Petipa's standing and whether he bestowed the gift of the undead upon her. Viktoria never speaks to Vincent of this event again.

Now to reveal to you Vincent and Viktoria's twining tale."

They all leapt as a noise vibrated from the window glass to the interior. Jürgen and Valerie ran to the pane instantaneously. Amanda kneeled to the floor with both hands to her chest. She had no color in her cheeks and appeared ready to be sickened.

Jürgen and Valerie presumed the striking object was akin to a bird as they did not see anything amiss. Their prayers went to that hope anyhow.

Amanda found her breath. Jürgen reached her slumped figure next. He kissed the tiny beads of perspiration from her forehead. She was cold and clammy. He wrapped himself around her as Valerie looked on in grave concern.

Chapter 30

Reviving Amanda

As soon as Jürgen and Valerie had begun tossing items together in order to vacate the premises, Amanda's revival was assured. Valerie packed for Amanda as Amanda felt her heart restore its pulse and the circulation of her blood. The cold and clammy feel, the weakness and the retching sense diminished. Anaphylaxis had fingered its way into her and its harmful effect had squeezed her less as she watched Jürgen and Valerie ready all so as to flee back to the more comforting confines of Calw and beyond.

Valerie had rushed to fetch Amanda a one serving size apple juice container, punched in the straw and insisted that Amanda drink. Amanda recalled the emergency preparedness course that the two of them had once taken together. Valerie must have been thinking of Amanda's sugar and electrolyte levels and the fact that apple juice was not about to roil her stomach in the process of restoring and raising those levels.

Amanda tested her knees to find their degree of strength. Her knees and legs worked perfectly without any unsteadiness. Her injured foot had shown no noticeable signs and symptoms of the prior injury for a while now. Distraction was the real healer she was finding.

She was avidly ready when the other two had paid the hotelier who was on duty and hoisted their bags into the auto.

"I am good as gold, Amanda, Valerie. I can drive into the dawn hours to make our exit. And I will be vigilant at the same time!"

Shortly after, Neubulach and surrounds were in their rearview mirror and were rapidly receding as they sped away. For Amanda, the vehicle could not go fast enough for her satisfaction. She knew, though, the combination of dark and a somewhat precarious road necessitated caution too. She trusted Jürgen's skill and judgment, Valerie's always also, maximally. But her sense of fear and urgency kept her feeling ill and weak.

When Amanda had finished the juice and it had been tolerated by her stomach, Valerie passed the water filled canteen to Amanda.

"Now that you are more relieved Amanda, should I finish the rendition or leave you time to more completely recover?"

"That is sweet and considerate of you to ask her, Jürgen," Valerie interjected.

Amanda glanced rearward at Valerie and smiled. As Valerie returned that smile with one of her own, instincts absolutely attuned to each other, Amanda laid her palm on Jürgen's thigh. "I love you, Jürgen. You have been and are wonderful."

"I love you too most beautiful woman. You are a gift and a gift to me."

Valerie softly added, "My Jeffrey would agree with the true grace of your shared love. And I would applaud him one hundred percent."

Amanda cherished Valerie.

And she continued. "I am recovering from the hotel room and I am even beginning to recover from my sadness regarding Marius."

"He is to be frightened of Manda, love. We all might be threatened as we speak. Please replace that image of his shine in your heart right now with realism no matter the effort. Promise me that!" Valerie was insistent.

"That has happened inside of me now my friend. It surprises me but I have no more illusions regarding Marius. And, Jürgen, I have sure faith in your decision as to how to proceed. I am ready to hear the remainder if you are ready as well."

He placed his hand upon hers and said, "I am ready while it is still fresh upon me."

"Then reveal it to us please."

Valerie leaned in to hear everything as Jürgen spoke. "Yes, how do the odd Vincent and fine Viktoria come together? He is her guardian and her lover simultaneously. Here is how that mismatch seems to have developed. Oddly also, my instincts tell me that Viktoria is as enamored of Vincent equal to Vincent's passion for her. Emotions have their unique path is all that I can guess there.

Well, when whatever calamity explodes between Petipa and Viktoria, Viktoria leaves Marius, St. Petersburg and Russia in a single action. And she does not have to plod to her destination. According to Vincent, as would make sense, she uses her new powers automatically.

Ah ha! So, without a doubt, he is vampire and he must have turned her. When turned, she is capable of flight, as a bat, per the ever scribbling Vincent. So, for whatever reason, Petipa bites her and rouses her undead powers; it can be by no other method.

Plainly put, without a question in my mind, your Marius, Amanda, is Petipa and a vampire.

Amanda blurted, "He spared me though! Even if I love him no more, he did do that!"

Valerie looked as perplexed as Amanda was by this fact.

"Thank God for that my precious love. Whatever Marius's reason, God stood over you then! May God see us through this too?"

Amanda clutched his hand tightly and her eyes shimmered in the glow of her love for him. She whipped his mouth to hers for a blink, kissed him profoundly and then gently twisted his head back to the roadway.

"You are my amazing Amanda."

Valerie's grin was unstoppable.

Chapter 31
NOT OCCUPIED

"Back to Viktoria though. She chooses some familiar territory to come home to. She takes her chances and returns to her family's cottage. It is intact in structure but has deteriorated while vacant. She is resourceful and over a difficult to distinguish period, she restores part of it to an order that she prefers.

Vincent never mentions why it is not occupied but my thought there is that the mine is producing much less silver by then and the operation shrinks and that means that the cottage is no longer needed.

If you think this has been bizarre so far, in spite of chopped and seemingly missing pages, the remainder outdoes itself!"

Amanda shut her eyes against the passing woods dark mystery and Valerie kept her head as close to the front seat as possible; the nearer the better for a multitude of reasons.

"Do you recall the second cottage in the woods? The cottage whose trail sank sharply into the forest core? Four people subsist there as Viktoria abides in her own dwelling. It is a family with both parents and a male and a female child.

The father is a woodcutter named Juria. The stepmother is Claire. The children, crazy, crazy stuff here, are Hansel and Gretel of Brother's Grimm fame."

Both Amanda and Valerie shuddered in the auto's warm interior.

"I open my arms to Seattle immediately. I have to get out of Germany. Val and I have return tickets. We will find a quick flight from Stuttgart to Seattle as soon as we arrive there. Jürgen, you will accompany us on that return flight. Val and I will wait until three seats on the same plane are available.

This is just too frighteningly outlandish to bear further!"

Valerie prompted Jürgen to conclude what was developing into a too wild and scary concoction of events. "Get it done, Jürgen! No more lingering amongst the drama. Spit the remainder out pronto dear boy!"

Amanda now sat with legs crossed underneath her. Her upper body curled as if in a cocoon. Jürgen's hand blanched as she unconsciously gripped his palm strongly.

"Yes, you are correct Valerie. Amanda, I apologize much. This last though is extremely difficult to piece together. The upshot as I figure it is that there is a crisis where Hansel and Gretel go lost, taken, kidnapped or something. Viktoria and the parents, Juria and Claire, ally jointly in their hunt for the children.

Not only does it become garbled here but it appears to be a complex set of events. The gist that I am able to tease out is that the young Hansel and Gretel have been taken by a being or beings unknown to the trio. Vincent bypasses many facts so I have no accounting for why the three even unite in their desire to save Hansel and Gretel. Viktoria is a vampire after all. Why would she do other than feed on blood?

Not only that, but then, as if pages are misplaced, an entire portion of happenings go missing. There is a page or two that describe Vincent's role as guardian to Claire."

"You have to be mistaken, Jürgen. You expressed to us that Vincent is Viktoria's guardian. What of that?" Valerie queried.

Amanda sat as if paralyzed by it all.

"I do not know. Maybe he was everyone's guardian. I am as confused as you are. The final page is commonplace for Vincent as he ruminates on his and Viktoria's blended heat. Then everything ceases.

I can guess but you and Amanda are now as informed as I am."

Amanda cried out, "Hansel and Gretel are a goddamned fairy tale and vampires are only legend!"

Everyone fell silent after Amanda's potent declaration.

The night sky was sweeping itself away as the hum of tires on asphalt kept susurrating through the vehicle's chassis to their ears.

The stress and tension were palpable.

Valerie dropped into a doze.

Amanda moved and lay horizontally with legs yet curled and head against Jürgen's jeans. She whispered but knew that he heard her, "Meeting you is the only real blessing of this trip." Then she too slept.

Calw was rearward and the Black Forest was behind them at this hour. Jürgen was obliterated from fatigue but soldiered on toward Stuttgart.

Nearing the airport, Amanda woke and pushed herself upright. "I have not been helpful much since our trek to the one cottage. I owe you an apology there. I just feel emotionally beat. Our love is what keeps me afloat. I am aware that being in Seattle is no magic bullet either. Marius is there, not in Germany as far as we know. But my mother, in particular, is waiting to welcome me home. It will feel so comforting and secure to have her near me again.

I desire that they meet you my love. They will be spellbound just as I am.

It is also time for Val to reconnect with Jeffrey. They have been apart long enough."

Jürgen stroked her hair repeatedly as she spoke to him. He had talked so much since their leaving the trail head that he cared merely to immerse himself in Amanda's warmth and whatever words she chose to direct his way.

As they pulled into the car rental area of the airport, Jürgen parked. Valerie hung in a dream in the backseat. So he took this fleeting opportunity to bend into Amanda and kiss her lips softly and passionately. He loved her ever so much.

Chapter 32

HOPE'S CARESS

The human race was so arrogantly self-centered. This opinion of his was bedrock and never to be anything but that. A human being was driven to view what frightened them as evil without nuances. They exhibited no compassion when the unknown or a close approximate of that confronted them.

His reflection went to himself, of course. As a vampire, only fellow creatures had a true understanding of one another. Other vampires were cognizant of undead frailties because they lived those frailties.

Not humans though. In order to fight their dreads, build energy in pursuit of defeating their supposed opposition, they distorted their facts to serve their aggressive purposes. A vampire to them became twisted, two dimensional, shallow and without feelings; only human's possessed feelings. And this was finally riling Marius to a level of anger such that he became self-protective in regards to Amanda.

She had been absent for what seemed an eternity, even to him. He loved her and he missed her fiercely. He hurt as a human hurt.

He resisted his undead psychic powers no longer. His abilities to view others physically, mentally and emotionally were thorough and fantastic. He had cultivated the ability for centuries and, in the process, it had become a mighty tool for him in his arsenal of undead tools.

He did wield that tool, those tools, as an instrument of good. Laugh at this humans, he inwardly scoffed. The idea of a mostly benign and empathetic vampire, well, how absurd an idea a person was most likely to think; and, equally, how wrong they would be in their sliver-thin assumptions. Marius had contributed positively to human society frequently as more than merely the Petipa incarnation.

Damn people!

Anyhow, pulling his reflections back to Amanda, it was also well within his command to block his and other vampire's ability in that all-seeing, all-knowing capacity.

He was the undead king of abilities; his age reached out to the murkier recesses of early antiquity. So, without undue difficulty, he had shielded himself from viewing Amanda's actions since her suspicions of him had begun.

Ironic in that the human supposition for his actions was that he should have probed Amanda and manipulated her, or simply killed her, in his self-interests. With Amanda, he was simply not capable of that. It just was not who he was.

Human's had no genuine comprehension of a vampire's essence and faculties. A short list of misguided human notions here: a vampire had no heart for love; a vampire suffered no anguish that their undead impulse to feed was uncontrolled and incontrovertible. Little ideas also were false. The one that dashed into his mind at this moment was the fabrication that vampire's had to be invited in before they were able to enter. To use human terms, what hogwash!

He loved Amanda as he had loved Viktoria. And he had been ashamed when he had inadvertently transformed Viktoria into one of his kind. She had loathed him from then on. Unbeknownst to her though, as he had walled off her vision of him, he followed and protected her from the instant that she had exited St. Petersburg.

And he grew determined to never enter this folly with Viktoria with any other person that he profoundly loved. And that was most certainly as it was with Amanda. As soon as his blood lust became imminent, he was hugely impatient to rush her away. She had to be shielded from him by him. There was no alternative course if Amanda's life was to be preserved.

He recalled the night where he had pecked her on the neck as he had seen to her departure. He had almost done a deed in his hard hunger that he would have forever regretted had it been accomplished. Both Amanda and Viktoria would have been on his conscience forever then.

Ironically, Amanda comprehended not at all that she need never be frightened of him. If she had been aware, she would not have reacted against him ever.

Of necessity, he spent little time with Amanda outside of their Giselle. His manufactured excuses must have seemed false to her eventually.

Eventually was now upon him. He had to project into her space immediately. His every sense spoke to him of his heightening peril.

So he peered into all that had and was happening in Germany since Amanda had arrived there.

He found that her heart had bound itself to another in this short period. He let it impact him. A piece of him recognized that as the best occurrence for her. Yet an entirely separate piece of his never corrupted spirit compressed in sadness and immortal tears; tears that did not stream down his face but did cascade through his heart.

He had also promised himself that he was not ever going to meddle with or manipulate Amanda's life events. With power, he had to, wanted to, temper that with some reason, some wisdom. Therefore, he chose to let nature take its course when he could and as often as able with those whom he loved. He left Amanda alone then to form the course of her life. Immortal maybe, God he was not!

He was to always wish her well.

However, he was aware since turning his psychic abilities on her moments ago, that Amanda was not probably ever going to wish him well.

On a lesser plane, Giselle's opening night had been a fine success and he estimated that his services were no longer really required. He, just as with Amanda, had a second. And she was as competent as was Rebecca. The show would go on in a splendid manner.

And so he fled in a rush as he recognized that Amanda and her companions were in flight at this very second; he ought to be in flight soonest also.

He had permitted hope's caress to determine his destination upon his own departure. He desired that someone or something in this infinite universe wished him well.

Without any more deliberations, ruminations, philoso-phizing or devastating probes, he took to the bright moon's company and winged his way away from Seattle.

Chapter 33

HOME'S PULL

Now that their flight had arrived on the tarmac through the thick clouds of the developing storm and its associated wind, Valerie relaxed considerably.

They had persuaded the Stuttgart ticket taker to redo, for an additional fee of course, her and Amanda's tickets but to additionally seat Jürgen directly across the aisle from them. Their predawn departure had worked in their favor as a nearly empty flight to Seattle, via New York, had emerged. It was such a fortunate happening and Valerie, quite cautious yet, felt blessed. It seemed to have been the difference between Amanda's psychological implosion as opposed to her reestablished confidence. Bottom-line she truly believed, Amanda's restored sense of love in Jürgen and his very clear return of that to her, gave Amanda a fundamental solace that was unique. It girded her even in her weakest periods. It was more than strong, it was lifesaving.

They had been so rushed to enplane in Stuttgart and were virtually passed out while they waited for their flight to leave New York, that they had not alerted Amanda's family, Jeffrey or anyone else to their arrival. That deep fatigue had caused them all to sleep the flight away with Jürgen's head facing the women and she and Amanda holding hands. It had not occurred to them, thus, to phone anyone.

As they deplaned into the guts of the Seattle terminal, they chattered mindlessly, contentedly and principally about the welcome dark and churning weather in the Pacific Northwest. Outsiders were often perplexed but, and this greatly amused Valerie, the country bumpkins of this out of the way region were very fond of, as Jürgen would rapidly learn, their frequent rain and slate gray skies. One was not a true member of their habitat if they did not enjoy bundling up, counting raindrops and imagining fantastic potentials for the shapes of the multitudinous clouds. This was home's pull and they relished it.

There was a point then where they seated themselves in an airport fast food joint. Valerie pressed them to discuss strategy between sweet bites of food; although in Jürgen's case, it was huge chunks of the stuff swallowed ravenously. "I want to lay out my ideas for our next steps."

"Couldn't we just give it all up, Val?" Amanda plaintively moaned.

"I can guess what Valerie has in mind. But tell us." Jürgen exclaimed.

"Marius is dangerous and I understand your need, Manda, to leave well enough alone. But for all of our sake's now, and I am aware of its risk too, we need to restore Viktoria's photograph to its original place.

I do not wish Marius to discover that it has disappeared. That would very likely encourage his wrath!"

"Exactly." muttered Jürgen.

"But Val, how would he recognize who to direct his wrath toward?" Amanda did not choose to return to his house under almost any circumstances.

"He resorts to simplicity. He lists those who have been in his abode recently. And he pursues them all. Sort of a scorched earth approach, you see."

"And I would be prominent on that list, yes?"

"You are very correct, sweet Manda; and by association, Jürgen and me too.

The three of us presume that his being undead is fact. That means, being accurate, we are safely free to enter in the light of day."

"My next question to you Val is this. What if he has replaced his locks? That seems enormously logical to me. Then we are helpless to investigate."

"I pondered that likelihood while you two drowsed, and drowsed and then drowsed some more."

They all chuckled at Valerie's accuracy.

"Then we give up, return to our routines, Jürgen gets introduced to all and we stay alert and hope for the best.

I do not desire to stake our odds on a hope and a prayer though. My instincts resound with this belief, that when I accidentally stumbled upon Viktoria's photograph, it appeared as if its positioning had gone undisturbed at length. Once in hand, I even swiped a thin layer of dust from its surface. He must think that it is safe.

I doubt that he has checked its presence or absence while we were off on our foray. The locks have not been changed. I sense that absolutely.

And, if I am incorrect, we fall back on the hope and a prayer plan and keep our guard up intensively."

"Amanda, when we get Valerie's auto and we drive to his residence, you remain in the car and act as spotter. That way, you will remain unscathed." Jürgen spoke this as he was genuinely eager for Amanda's utmost protection.

Amanda was not having that at all. "I go where the two of you go. We share hazards equally. Jürgen, I love you and thank you for your sensitivity towards me, but no, I enter his home side by side as three.

You, Val, have convinced me. We will replace the photograph behind the pendulum."

They hurried from their table to grapple with their luggage and then hail a cab for their ride to Valerie's.

Valerie decided silently that if Jeffrey were at home upon their arrival, she would persuade him to become their lookout. The prospect of his being there was reed-thin.

She guessed that he was hard pounding the computer at his job.

Valerie, thorough thinker that she was, accurately assessed the situation regarding Jeffrey. She was willing to add his presence if she had been forced to. He was not there and she was not compelled to spell out the assumed truth of Marius yet. She did not want the complications of his concern at this moment. She was anxious to do the deed and depart.

They sat hushed in her vehicle as they approached Marius's neighborhood. And that was even with post dawn brightness surrounding them. Fears, as was more than reasonable, remained much heightened.

Chapter 34

ELEGANTLY UNEXPECTED

The key fit beautifully in the lock below and the lock above. The deadbolt thumped open and Amanda paced into the interior with Jürgen and Valerie close behind. To his proximate neighbors, Jürgen surmised, it was Amanda visiting Marius with two friends in tow. The benign and casual look of that was perfect for their purposes.

As soon as they were in the living room, Valerie harshly whispered, "Jesus! He has to have a basement for his sarcophagus. Amanda, were you ever aware of a basement in this house?"

"I did not pay much attention to it but, no, I always presumed that it was a single level structure."

"Again, I stake my life on the fact that, as with the key just used fitting both locks, the solution to locating his casket's whereabouts is as elementary as it is unexpected.

Amanda, Jürgen, think fast and hard here!"

Jürgen instantly retorted, "Easily solved I believe. You suggest the elegantly simple and unexpected for Marius's resting place. You also suggest that this is certainly solvable with other than the usual perspective?"

"Yes, yes, Jürgen. What have you supposed?" Amanda marveled at Jürgen's mental dexterity, especially if he had the solution to this riddle. Jürgen knew this and was pleased.

"Marius requires that for daylight hours he not be found. As a vampire, he might perish if his tomb were located. It is of exquisite importance to him then that it is deeply hidden in plain sight.

What is an alternative form for a vampire? The most prominent is that of a bat. Bats fly, they elevate into the sky. So the undead, Marius, minds neither depths nor heights. And, though the stereotype of vampires automatically triggers the image of a coffin protected deep in the ground, what is above the main floor that every house possesses and that a being unafraid of heights might use?"

Amanda and Valerie, in unison, mouthed to the other, "the attic."

"Follow me this way and I will show you both the square in the ceiling where I am positive that the attic opening is."

"Wait! Punch these under his left nipple if need be! The heart beats strongest there." Valerie grabbed stainless steel knives from their holder and spread them on the kitchen counter top. Amanda and Jürgen each took one after Valerie took hers.

Now armed, they bounded after Amanda. When Amanda pointed to the inset lines in the hallway ceiling, Jürgen rushed to position a chair beneath. He raised the large panel and grasped the folding set of stair steps.

Jürgen lowered those steps carefully and used them silently. He mounted the finished attic flooring and spied the long and narrow polished container. The lid was upright.

He had not expected this. Why was it such? All was hushed in the attic's shadows. He sensed empty space exclusively. He held a moment longer and then charged the casket, knife arched aloft.

It was empty; dirt and dirt alone was inside the contraption. His eyes skimmed the attic's confines in a last sweep. Again, there was silence and nothing else.

He dropped to the hallway carpeting without using the steps. He heaved the stairs upward and once those steps sank into place, the attic panel automatically fell to and almost blended with the hallway ceiling.

"He has departed. The casket is empty and the attic is completely abandoned.""

"He was in a hurry I would think as his belongings all remain as always." Amanda took another look as final assurance of her statement.

"There is our proof then. Between Vincent's pages and the existence of his casket, Marius can disguise himself no longer." Jürgen felt confident of this.

Valerie quickly interjected. "I am no attorney but this would not constitute proof in a court of law. I say that because we do not have incontrovertible proof yet. What we have is circumstantial evidence. It is strong evidence that vampires and other demons actually exist. Yet we need a link or two more to tie it to Marius.

Strangely, we have not cemented Marius individually to his being a vampire. We believe that he is without a shadow of a doubt. But would our evidence be convincing enough to others? Vincent never figured who transformed Viktoria for sure. The casket, though the thought is ludicrous to us, could belong to anyone. That does not make for an airtight case."

Jürgen would have laughed at the pun had Valerie not been so serious.

"Let's replace the photograph and scour the house one more time for clues that we may have missed. If Marius does reappear, his precious photograph of Viktoria will not create suspicion."

Long ago, Jürgen had passed Viktoria's tiny portrait back to Amanda. She clutched at the ancient clock as she readied to restore the photograph to its proper prior status behind the pendulum front. As she stepped back from the mantle, her heel caught on a perfectly blended tiny throw rug beneath her and she bounced to the carpet with the clock sent curving through the air.

The smack of the clock was distinct. Amanda grimaced; not, probably, at any pain to her but at the remnants of the timepiece. Now it meant there was nothing to return the photograph to. The clock seemed shattered. Even its backside had popped from its position.

A tiny book stared all of them in the face. It was askew as it peeped from what remained of the false wooded back.

Chapter 35
AVERTED DISASTER

The threads of the cloth binding were visible and divided one from the other at its back base. It projected from Marius's clock so she presumed that it was Marius's book too. But wait, Amanda considered; it being his clock did not absolutely mean that it was his book. She still was moved to bestow a rare gentleness upon Marius. No more of that! This was his book!

As she scrambled for the prized article, her mind flickered to wonderment at why he had used two locations for his special photograph and this. Why not both in the safer false back? All that she salvaged of this thought was that he had cleverly split the two pieces so that any pursuers would have a much more challenging time of an entire rendering of Marius's story this way. If all the information had been deposited in a single spot, it was as if Marius were handing himself over to his trackers on a platter.

Really though, the greatest odds favored his conceit that no one was bright enough to sniff him out. And even if they did, his arrogance would assume their dullness and their incapacity to ever disentangle his deeds. Enlarging on this consideration, she concluded that the perfect solution was if he had kept those significant items on his person. Ego's carelessness was at work here.

How rapidly her resentment of Marius had escalated and her love had cratered. Each ticking second created an ill will toward him as her anger at his deceit grew.

All of these considerations marched through her brain in quick cadence, boom, boom, boom, as she reached for the object.

As Valerie and Jürgen dashed to her aid, Amanda blurted, "Look at this!"

She clutched the book and then slipped it to Valerie as she attempted to tidy up the mess. She double checked the false compartment and amazingly, successfully closed it as the spring lock snapped together. The front glass flap door to the device was open but fully intact. Maybe no obvious damage had been done to the antique. God, she hoped so!

Jürgen located the inadvertently fall-tossed photograph and waited while Amanda tested the time piece. Valerie unconsciously held her breath as Amanda walked the clock through its paces. It functioned flawlessly and appeared undisturbed. Disaster seemed to have been averted.

Jürgen gave Amanda the photograph and she reopened the beautiful filigreed front enclosure, delicately sealed the picture to the pendulum posterior, set the arm into side to side motion, reclosed all, studied it front and back and most carefully replaced it in its original position on the mantle. She even returned the small throw to its prior place, squared up, flattened out and seeming just right. Hallelujah, everything was situated and Valerie and Jürgen agreed that all was fine.

Amanda smacked her forehead and posed this, "It just occurred to me. We replaced the photograph but now have emptied the clock of the journal. Might he not notice that? What of that Val, Jürgen?"

Val and Jürgen said in unison, "Oh my God!"

After a seconds pause, Val continued by replying, "You are so right Manda! Here's the logic there as I see it. Mind you, this is on the spot thinking but I feel its solidity. This journal, if it exposes Marius incontrovertibly, as I believe that it will, has to remain in our hands or the public's hands as the pure evidence of his evil. He will not come after us then as we are no longer worthwhile as a consideration to him. He will see that he is already revealed and will stay in hiding wherever and forever."

Amanda asked Val a second query, "Val, you have the book?"

"Absolutely Manda, I am not about to let go of it!"

"Let's get the hell away from here then! Marius's home creeps me out now. I wish that it did not but it does."

They scurried through the main door after scanning the living room one last time and then primly entered Valerie's vehicle as if they had concluded a fine, friendly and routine chat with Marius. The neighbors certainly were not about to be suspicious at this sight.

"I thought we were done in when you tripped, Manda."

"I so thought the same until I glimpsed the book. Then I let all distractions disappear and went on autopilot. Usually, I cannot put anything back together once it is apart."

Jürgen was excited. "Reading that book might be a godsend. We need to find a safe place to skim it to begin!"

"I never can tell when my roomie might appear at her and my apartment," Amanda volunteered.

"That is too true, Manda. Sally can be very unpredictable.

It still is many hours before Jeffrey is off of work. My house is the logical destination then." Valerie aimed the auto towards her and Jeffrey's residence. They had a study that Jeffrey principally used. He never locked it but it had that capacity. A bit much conceivably but safety was paramount, especially if this book were worth something to them in their investigation.

Valerie had passed the tome baton-like to Amanda as Valerie had scooted behind the steering wheel. Amanda hesitated to open it as if it were likely to attack her once beheld; a Pandora's Box of starkly harmful information.

Jürgen cautioned from the backseat, "Secure it on your person Amanda until we are tucked away in Valerie's house. That may sound excessive but is probably our smartest approach right now."

They did just that.

They stole into the study and clicked the lock shut. They were able to relax and felt the snugness of the well-worn room. This was a cave that Jeffrey used frequently, Amanda understood.

Flat on the carpet, feet crossed in the air similar to children, prone lying, they formed a circle around their target. Amanda reached for it and touched the heavy cover gingerly. "You may do the honors, Jürgen."

She rotated the tome his way and he opened the heavy cover without hesitation.

"It is in his hand! Marius always writes in those bold flares and ostentatious loops at the ends of words." Amanda was sure of that.

Yet she was unsure of the rest. "Jürgen, what would we do if you had not joined in this?"

"And missed finding you? Never!" Jürgen stretched and kissed Amanda firmly on her lips. She stretched into that tender touch avidly.

"German script it is again. It was Vincent first and now it is Marius."

Jürgen read it aloud to them.

It took several hours.

Chapter 36

FORBIDDEN TOME

It began with the heading, "This, My Forbidden Tome." It was signed in the single word name of Marius.

As the read words spun to Valerie's ears, she had to ask herself as to why he would write that which, though only briefly, puts the brand of vampire upon himself? And further, no wonder he also called it "Forbidden". It was the truth be told; his true tale as well as Hansel and Gretel's. In that, though inexplicably composed and then not destroyed, he had had to suppress it at all costs.

As Jürgen poured through the days and nights of Marius's reckoning, Valerie heard the book manifest itself as a journal of his that spanned the period directly after Viktoria's abandonment of him; when he was yet most sickly in love with her and freshly abashed at his errant misstep between them. He was captive to his heart and it was almost unique thus far in his undead life. Valerie nearly wept for him until she recalled what he was.

Valerie felt his effort to be objective even as it must have tormented him. His ability to envision Viktoria's every nuance, thoughts, actions, yearnings, were powerful, she guessed, in order for him to protect her. He became

Viktoria's unknown guardian, she surmised. Though, ironically, Viktoria was the last being on the face of the earth requiring protection. She was a force unto her own.

Valerie failed still to comprehend his putting pen to paper at all though.

There were several segments of his tome that fascinated her particularly. Simultaneously, she was pondering its effect upon Jürgen and Amanda.

According to Marius, and his writing was more than persuasive, it read as fact, was fact, Hansel and Gretel were not a fiction out of the Brothers Grimm imaginations but were alive, innocent, precious and hugely imperiled while separate from their father and stepmother. This stepmother of theirs, Claire, loved them as they loved her. Wicked and hateful of the children she was not. Actually, she was absolutely the polar opposite of that! Animosity between them was so nonexistent within the bond that she loved Hansel and Gretel equally with her lover and husband, Juria. When the children disappeared, Hansel and Gretel meant everything to both of them. They required their innocent young ones intact so as not to feel destitute. Juria, a common woodcutter married twice, and Claire, manor born and beautiful, despaired in their desperate pursuit through the forest for his offspring.

Then there was the most peculiar alliance of Claire and Juria with Viktoria. That Viktoria aided the sweet and frightened pair in their plight was a marvel to behold. And Viktoria's reasons for rendering this assistance were most remarkable.

That Claire and Juria were persuaded to believe her was even more astounding.

The truly devilishly incomprehensible happened when Viktoria launched Claire and Juria into a sexual threesome with her. Was this due fully to awesome strength as a demon? Valerie thought not! Juria and Claire were captivated from the moment of watching the spectacle of Viktoria change from bat to entirely ravishing woman.

The intimate entangling was seemingly spontaneous, yet the seed had already been planted and passionate for the colluding three. Even Viktoria had yielded to the mighty force of its electric pleasures. That Viktoria did not suck their lives away from them, well, miracles honestly did occur.

Valerie substituted herself for Claire in that ménage. Would any detail have been different? She thrilled to the idea of, having seen Viktoria just come from Claire's tongue, coming again and again with the supine Viktoria. She would stare Viktoria in the eyes while licking her thick and sensitive dark nipples. She would watch Viktoria's aureoles constrict, thereby her nipples lengthened. Both were vivid cravings for Valerie. She therefore experienced a wetting of her sex instantly. She desired plunging fingers into her opening immediately but was not about to. Her growing lust would have to be satisfied later. She did continue with the fantasy for a bit longer though.

Valerie thrilled more deeply at the idea of pressing Viktoria's legs apart then and grazing her lips over Viktoria's belly until she arrived at her scorching nether region; to spread

Viktoria's lips there and draw voraciously at Viktoria's reloaded clit until Viktoria writhed and pounded wave upon wave into Valerie's mouth.

Valerie pictured a surge so long and dominant in Viktoria that Valerie was even able to hold Viktoria in place as light of day struck her. What sizzling domination was that, Valerie concluded!

Valerie, though she did not aspire to be intimate with any female, was incited to the point of heat at this particular image that she considered participation in intertwined passion between herself, Jeffrey and one other gorgeous female.

Vincent was involved often throughout and Valerie had to believe that Jürgen eased his notion of Vincent as a simpleton with undeserved pretenses toward sophistication. Vincent was obviously wonderfully unique and of a complex nature. Valerie was rocked by empathy for him moment to moment.

Marius must have quaked as he documented all. Vincent and Viktoria's passion for one another, the heated exchange of the threesome and Viktoria's initiation and then submission to it, Viktoria's very rare recollections of Marius must have been shattering. His emotional survival had to have depended upon his undead existence to blunt the pain.

Vincent had evolved so often. His metamorphosis flowed from lout, to farm owner, onward to werewolf, then to protector of Claire and finally guardian and lover of Viktoria.

His notes, found at Viktoria's cottage, were poetic. Valerie reminisced on this as Jürgen's words danced upon her senses.

Again, how did this stir Amanda and Jürgen? What of the grandeur of Claire's parent's manor, or their feelings at the enormity of Viktoria and Vincent's last recorded coupling?

Questions swamped her.

Jürgen finished.

It was the incontrovertible evidence required.

Chapter 37
Five O'clock News

Jeffrey remained absent and this gave the trio time to discuss their options without having to explain or unload it on a fourth.

"That fills in every gap in this entire search, chronology and all. I am stunned at the implications here, not just for us, but for people in general!"

"And between his tome, Amanda, his casket and Vincent's pages, we have all the pieces to provide proof positive. These tell of the authenticity of the existence of vampires and werewolves in general, Marius as a vampire himself and less importantly, though stunningly, that fairy tales are not always tales. This is profound and frighteningly outrageous evidence."

Jürgen bludgeoned the other two with this swift and concise analysis.

"Further, if this were fiction, I would still be moved. And periodically, it feels surreal that it is anything other than fiction. But we know that it is the genuine goods and it insists on the reality of our being perpetually surrounded by grave threats. It is ghastly and beyond impacting just us." Jürgen broke a sweat for the very first time since having met Amanda.

"But there was different than threat in all that we have discovered. None of us have been injured or have even been confronted with violence in this very trying journey of ours. There is an underbelly of softness here; and if not softness, humanness then."

That raised a slight chuckle briefly all around.

"Human they are not." Jürgen exclaimed.

"Well, there are more than just traces of humanness amongst them. Vincent is clearly not a monster. Viktoria is often ashamed of her fatal impulses and undead nature.

And you, Manda, were in love with Marius.

What makes sense here?"

Valerie's defense of beasts surprised Amanda. It had been Valerie who had sought the striping of Marius's exterior to gain greater insight into him more than anyone; definitely more than her. Possibly Valerie and Jürgen had been equally predisposed to push onward.

Nevertheless, Amanda disagreed with her fine friend. So she countered Valerie's argument by saying, "There was chronic uncertainty on our parts as to whether we would be attacked during our honest pursuit of the truth. That is neither reasonable nor right. Evil fears transparency or the light of day.

And I did love Marius. Yet I did not know him remotely then.

I am frightened. And we have to alert others so that they can defend themselves if the need arises against a potential bloodletting of their own.

And, ultimately, there is no denying that vampires feed off of blood, animal or human. If not our blood, then it has been someone else's. And we have to stand against that! All of the creature's good intentions are buried by this drive of theirs.

I vote to take every shred of information that we have gathered and take it to the most liberal and understanding news station in Seattle."

"Valerie, I have to say that I agree wholeheartedly with Amanda. I have been drawn toward leniency after having experienced Marius's words. But I will not be blinded by their potential for tender emotion. My opinion follows Juria's as well as Amanda's. A vampire's bloodlust and uncontrolled annihilation of life says it all for me." Jürgen had said his piece.

"Val, time to decide upon which five o'clock news is best for the spread of our evidence. Actually, let's decide that as we drive."

"Manda, Jürgen, I am wrong and you are correct. I mellowed there for an instant. And that could be ruinous. Surely, the vampire lulls one into a sense of wellbeing and then suddenly feeds. Nope, I will not be a victim."

Let's head out."

Amanda understood that the clincher for the news people was not the written material but the sight of the empty casket in Marius's attic. They took a sizeable risk as one reporter accompanied Amanda, Valerie and Jürgen into the silent house. They had not knocked but had calmly entered as the trio had entered before.

The silence was dense.

The attached ladder was lowered and Jürgen led the reporter through to the attic.

Amanda imagined that the reporter feared the illegality of their presence more than he was alarmed at the potential presence of vampires. She assumed that he did not have huge hope that this story was real. He had gone on the stern command of his supervisor. So he must have been stunned when he was confronted with the empty but dirt filled casket. She was able to hear as he took shot after shot of the casket and the attic area. When he reappeared and showed her and Valerie the photographs of the intricately crafted and finely polished box, the women were speechless as well.

The entire enclosed environment of the attic spooked the reporter thoroughly he told them.

He was in a deep hurry to leave as soon as he had displayed the results of his work to the women. Jürgen simply observed from a distance.

Amanda easily guessed that the reporter was so relieved when they walked through to the hallways of the news station.

He exhibited his digital shots to his supervisor, his editor.

The editor did not react in any manner except that his pupils became huge.

Chapter 38

Outlook Change

He was apprised of the details as she understood them to be.

And he took her in his arms, enfolded her tightly, steadily, and next they rested heads on one another's shoulders. It was performed slowly, fondly initially and then so lovingly as it lasted.

He was foolish to have permitted her departure. He had most certainly not fathomed the depth of peril to her and thus was so fraught with tenderness for her while she nestled safely within his clasp. How sweet it was to be joined with the one you cherished like no other.

Jeffrey delicately moved aside a wisp of her hair that had strayed over her forehead and caught in her lashes.

He gentled these words to her while still in one armed embrace, "You, my precious wife, are, thankfully, here with me now."

He circularly stroked between her scapulae at upper spine without conscious attention to his soothing touch there.

"If you had recognized the menace of the situation and still had left, I would consider that reckless in spite of your concern for Amanda. You were unaware and have blessedly returned to me whole and unhurt.

Giving up your evidence to the media was beyond wise, my love. Val, it safeguards potential victims from calamity and death possibly. Marius will not reappear ever in Seattle again I would presume. His cover has been blown without doubt.

Your instincts about Marius were spot on Val."

"Jeff, in the interim, while I was gone, I have had a change in outlook. Your and my marriage came into a hard focus there. And I compared it to where my wanderlust led me.

Events in Germany terrified me. And with each successive dose of fear, especially as the bird struck the window, my heart went to you. Your beloved image comforted me no end. As a matter of fact, I was not able to settle emotionally each time until I conjured up your loving face speaking words of reassurance and support here." She stepped back from him a single pace and tapped below her left breast.

She peered up at his slightly glistening eyes, acted as if to dab at his not yet formed tears and kissed him. The kiss lost contact gradually until only the most tenuous of seal at lower lips was maintained and then separated naturally.

Jeffrey was going to have more of her.

Thoughts raced first though.

Her absence had struck him this occasion. Her essence had clung to him much more than usual. The sense of proximity for him had been kinetic this time, as if she had never left. Was this one of those watershed moments in their lives he wondered?

He had a longing for his Valerie only; no one else regardless of what he had mentioned in their discussion those several years ago. Her healthy spirit fascinated him. Her need to share material and immaterial sustenance with everyone captivated him. He lived the sense that he had been bestowed a gift in her.

With patience, he intuited, she would shed her intimate junkets that did not include him. For their love, he would endure. And he sensed that the enduring might finally be coming to an end.

So he took her and she let him.

He led to begin while she passively opened herself to his exploration of her. This was rare, he appreciated. Typically, she dominated as if she were an overconfident symphony conductor. The symphony portion always played well while the assertion and command sometimes did not for him.

He was to assert his manhood tonight and she willingly chose to follow.

He released all touch from her and motioned for her to remove her clothing. "You are so beautiful," he complimented. And she was. His affirmation of her was void of insincerity; he spoke truth to her beauty consistently.

As she leisurely shed her favorite white tank top for him, he too removed his jeans for her. "Leave your thong on gorgeous one," he told her. She responded exactly as he requested.

She was standing to his sitting now. As he requested, she would leave her crimson thong on. It, after all, matched her auburn hair color and assertive personality so naturally.

As she reached to undo her clasps, Jeffrey gazed at her intently. This was a very delicious moment for him in their intimacy. She never failed to please him at exposure of her large and perfectly hung breasts. They spilled forward as if readymade to settle into his awaiting cupped hands. That was to come in but a moment.

He sought to attempt a new approach first. He had swung his already long cock from its enclosure within his underwear out through the material's circle nearest his thigh. The elastic band there was to heighten his pulse from the extra pressure that this improvised cock ring would deliver.

He stroked his prominently veined, thick and throbbing rod before her. A clear dew drop formed at the opening of his red rounded cockhead.

He locked eyes with her as he slowly pumped his rod up and down for her. He stopped occasionally and squeezed it hard but did not otherwise move his hands. His cock became even more massive then. She was not able to lock eyes with him as she had to dazedly gape at his tool.

"Come here love. Lick me while I continue."

She moved as if mesmerized and came to him.

He cupped her breasts then. He removed his hands from himself and began to thumb her hard and rubbery nipples. This, by itself, created a surge through his tube.

And then she kneeled at his groin and clutched his outsize shaft and sucked what she could of him into her mouth. Her cheeks bulged as she did this. She was incapable of taking him more than halfway.

She lashed her tongue violently over his meat. She wanted to engulf him and pleasure him without restraint.

He lifted her up and she moaned in the desire to stay upon his cock with her mouth.

He could see that she craved his clothing not completely removed. She lusted for his cock's extra size from the mild tourniquet pressure as well. But it was the instant for all of his clothing to be peeled away.

He positioned himself on his back fully nude. His cock was so solid and full in his passion for her. "I want you above me. Sit on my cock. Face me. Take all of it if you can."

Valerie carefully bent to him. She shifted her thong band to the side and then spread her drenched lips wide with her fingers. Her inner lips glistened in their wetness.

At first hint of her touch with the heat of his rounded cockhead, she groaned in the agony of her desire. His cockhead, then superheated shaft met her vaginal tunnel.

She knew it would hurt but went for it anyway. She had invited herself atop him often before but he had never invited her thus. It caused her to lose control. She pounded down upon him and did that harder and faster than she had ever done before. The pain blazed but then blended into a mix of sensation that roused her incredibly. Somehow the pain elevated the pleasure in a loop that seized her and she threw her head back in wild abandon.

Jeffrey managed to rhythmically compress her nipples as she pistoned so mindlessly hard and fast over his cock.

She froze. She gasped. As he felt her interior ripples massage his cock, he was shattered as she was shattered. He shot burst upon strong burst into her. They both groaned. He fell to his back. She collapsed into him and gently shook and wept simultaneously.

Chapter 39
Sweet Introduction

They were upstairs in her childhood bedroom giggling about how sweet and easy the family introductions had gone. They were about to freshen up for dinner. Jürgen was reciting the names of those members he had just met and even more distant members that he was to meet in the future. It seemed to go on and on.

"There is your very kind Mom, Betty. And then there is your Dad, Ray. He is a stern one, don't you think?"

"You and he will find common ground often. You are very intelligent, fearless and loving men. Am I wrong?"

"Not wrong at all! I am just surprised that he was so cavalier with his own daughter to support your travel to Europe by yourself!"

"He has faith and confidence in me. He hoped that I would learn the lesson of good choice in men and learn it to never forget it."

"And did you?"

"I chose you didn't I? I think that I was a prize pupil." She leaned into him so that they both tumbled onto her bed.

She worked the buttons of his shirt over, releasing each and every one of them methodically. "OK now, more names. Spit them out. I will try not to distract you too much."

He chuckled softly and replied, "I am already too distracted."

"Mmmmmm, not as distracted as you will be soon enough."

"Then I better be quick with those names."

"Yes, quickly now, sir."

She finished with his buttons and freed his shirttails from his waistband and belt with a whoosh of motion. She was not about to let him concentrate and she immediately honed in on a nipple of his with her mouth while also reaching a hand of hers to his nestled cock. She loved its size even when soft. She fingered over his cockhead and playfully squeezed his now much less flaccid flesh.

As he tweaked the outline of her tender nipple through thin silk with a forefinger he breathed out, "Yes, your brothers are, ummm, Doug and Stephen.

Your nipple tip feels electric babe. Mmmmmm, your touch on me is uncanny also."

"And my sister?" she minced as she drew back slightly from his nipple.

"Don't stop love! Yes, yes, Barbara. Beautiful Barbara but never as beautiful as my Amanda!"

He took his other forefinger to her second nipple and languished in the erotic sense of her tips stretching and firming. His cock, at her gently determined contact was pressing hard against her moving fingers, her warm palm and it was about to rip through the cotton of his briefs to speak heatedly to her about that naughty touch of hers. The amusing but sexy image caused his cock to jerk under her ministrations.

"I cannot think here babe but shouldn't we prepare ourselves for dinner?" He quivered with desire throughout as he asked this question of her.

Amanda laughed. "Oh but we are preparing for just that. We have undressed and will change into other items momentarily."

Upon uttering these saucy, spirited words, she made short order of that silk blouse of hers. She tugged it past her cascade of blond tresses and over her head, off her toned arms into the air. She did not care where it landed.

She was as insistent with her full but seamless bra. She simply lifted the cups and gleefully said, "Hold these while I unclasp myself." She understood that he could not wait to do just that.

Jürgen was in a trance and did exactly as she instructed. He reached for her breasts as they popped to his curving cupped and trembling hands. Her breasts, in motion, not in motion, created in him passions that made his usually considerable cock more outsize than he had ever experienced before her.

The pale skin of both mounds was an ivory color to match his dreams easily. There was the faintest of venous color aesthetically webbing into convergence at those gorgeously pink, large round aureoles. The contrast of her perfectly pendulous and hugely massed breasts with the beautiful light coral of her aureoles and thick nipples damned him to a life of lusting after her perpetually; even more so that these prominent mounds hung on a slender frame. She was ripe with delicious contrasts. And then her heart . . . But he lost sight of everything as his cock strained to her motions.

They only restrained themselves in a single manner here. Jürgen placed a hand upon Amanda's mouth to muffle her moans and he focused the best that he could, if that were possible, to be silent at their climax. Family dignity had to be preserved.

She spiraled down into a voluptuous whirlpool of breathtaking wonder and pleasure. She spun into this ecstatic delirium powerlessly. And then she felt him thrust his last, grind into her, hold and then shoot what seemed endless spurts against her core. Amanda's orgasmic spasms yielded stars in an ever expanding universe.

He brought her crashing inward and exploding outward.

She needed nothing more.

Dinner was replete with joy at her return to Seattle and her clear love of Jürgen. Other than that, she learned that Giselle had opened successfully without her.

Chapter 40

His Plea

His sensitivity was a remnant of a mysterious aspect of himself that remained elemental even as he wielded his overarching undead strength. His sensitivity had commanded that he mirror his love, Viktoria, and watch over her. Most vampires were not of such a love-sick nature. He had a very tender underbelly in that regard.

It was also the reason behind the writing of his forbidden tome, his journal revealing Viktoria's undead life and his position in that sphere of her being, which was essentially that of nonexistence. That the tome exposed him as a vampire was secondary to his need connected to her. He yearned to be near her at all times; most especially after their sudden falling out. Writing a journal regarding her, her activities, her hopes, her lust even, allowed him to sense that she was almost there with him. His pen to paper gave him an aura of bringing her presence immediately before him.

He did not choose to have her understand his weakness, his sensitivity, this passion for her. So he blocked her psychic view of him. He exercised his dominant capacities to keep her from being aware that he shadowed her as a slave would his master. Ostensibly, he pursued her to protect her; really he did that to protect himself. He was unable to bear their parting.

Finally, he had gathered the emotional wherewithal to leave her, though she did not even recognize that he was physically proximate to her ever, and he wended his way to the shores of North America. The Sound and its unique geography impressed him the most.

He was in hasty reversal it seemed now. And he came in such urgent motion that he abandoned all that sat in the house on Seattle's waterfront. The most significant of items still there were his casket, of course, his treasured ancient clock, Viktoria's always well restored photograph and the tome he had been compelled to author.

They can have it all he pondered as he arched through the skies at a blinding pace in order to arrive where he knew Viktoria to be on the earliest hour of darkness. He had always discerned her location and now his love torn heart and loss of Amanda impelled him back to one love that was to restore him to emotional sanity.

His plea to her was about to be persuasively overwhelming. Time had dampened her resentments and she yearned for a passion herself on a level that she saw between Juria and Claire perpetually. This was the consummately appropriate moment for the both of them. He swore by that notion!

His plan was to beg her forgiveness with every ounce of vigor that flowed through the heart of this hugely remorseful vampire.

Aside from his tenderness of emotion and his lack of control over a bloody appetite, Marius differed from God in that he could neither create nor observe the future in the present. His talent came in the form of a limited omniscience, an omniscience that extended into the here and now; barely more, nothing less. His capacities for observation and, thus, interference and manipulation entailed a degree of uncertainty; guesswork to a degree.

His paradox was that he coveted and feared his potential ever enlarging capabilities. That did not stop him from continuing to practice his skills intensively so that eventually even future visibility would not be so difficult. He would tremble then but he would go forth nonetheless. Mystery was meant to collapse and give way before him. He was driven to answer all questions and throw wide the doors to a universal landscape.

With long years of focus and development, other vampires, lesser vampires, were bound to achieve some of the same. He though was unique in his capacity for heightened undead powers; levels of power that were created unachievable for all other vampires. Ironically, it was not his power that rendered him best for leadership but his benevolence that made him most especially able to guide others.

He continued to stifle Viktoria's psychic senses. He selected surprise as his most effective tool in the sizeable arsenal that he carried with him. He assumed her to be increasingly malleable to his suasion if he dealt with an unprepared resistance on her part.

Night owned the dawn for many more hours. He planted himself on solid earth, recaptured human resemblance, inhaled deeply of the fragrance that the garden's rosebuds provided and strode toward Viktoria's motionless and turned form.

She was composed and in intensive study of the manor house. He was aware that she cherished this small domain of hers, Juria and Claire's. She drank it in. He appreciated that she considered this circle of buildings her shelter and safe haven. Vampire's required safe haven too as he felt the trepidation from having just departed his own.

Her surprise was magnificently real and, obviously, shocking for her as he embraced her from behind. His lips went quickly to her unguarded neck and in a definite embrace; he filled his hands from her straining bodice with her full and voluptuous breasts.

"My ever love Viktoria. It is I, Marius. I forever must apologize to you. Accept that apology and we always will be together."

She answered calmly now that seconds had passed, he had spoken and her nipples firmed, "I had hoped for this my Marius. I quit you in a plume of haste and ragged emotion.

The passing time has subdued my ambivalences and since, I have simply waited and endured. I had no choice in that. What I was able to control was my permitting the embers of our prior fire inside of me to reignite and rebuild.

I hold nothing against you. It has been thus for many years now. Once my heart reached past the rest of my more ignorant self and cried out for you, then I ceased all other sentiment and quieted my interior, waiting upon your return only.

And you are here at last."

Chapter 41

FULL CIRCLE

They looked at each other and burst out laughing in unison. How quaint it was to have two vampires holding hands while strolling in shadows throughout the grounds.

Viktoria was as if a young girl in first bloom and blush of the throes of adolescent passion. She almost skipped she was so gleeful. Where their palms met, his and her pulses synchronized and beat together insistently. She flushed at the idea of such an innocent and elemental touch between them arousing her to the heights that she now found herself in.

She was verging upon climax without foreplay or union of any kind except the long anticipated meld of his warm fingers interconnected with hers. Her vampire had absolutely deserted her temporarily and she was left with the luscious pounding within her chest and a luminosity that was unspeakably human and benign.

"I have it mapped well in my mind, gorgeous Viktoria, but I want you to lead me through the nooks and crannies of this fortress of yours."

She shyly whispered to Marius, "It is not mine alone. Claire and Juria will be anxious to know you upon my introduction."

"The perfume that I smell upon you this eve, my gorgeous one, is the scent of sorrow passing and the greater scent of joy emboldened. These delicate and wonderful fragrances of yours lick at my brain and bring me to our full circle where my love for you began. It began then and it begins again; hope past and hope present.

You, from moment one, have swept me to corners of my passionate being that I had no comprehension I was capable of. I love you sweet Viktoria. That feeling is profound and it is eternal. It is stronger than anything that I ever felt with Amanda. She is but a pale, pale ghost as I stand at the ready to fulfill you . . . and fulfill you some more."

She smiled gaily. "Let me show you the way then; my way in and amongst will transform into, not just my hideaway any longer, but rather our hideaway."

There was a perimeter of approximately eight structures that encircled them.

"My original bed, created for another but was never occupied by her, is in the basement of the guesthouse which butts up against the wine cellar. Once I established myself there, I have remained there.

In anticipation that you were to appear someday, and I had that faith, I dragged one of the many manor pine boxes, used for burial when staff were in abundance here, to the guesthouse bowels so that on that fateful night, tonight, we would lie side by side.

"So thoughtful of you, my love. So very wonderfully thoughtful of you.

And where are Juria and Claire residing?"

"They stay, when at rest, within the lower confines of the manor house. It is huge and elegant throughout; baroque and not overly ornate. Claire especially warms to that. Juria's tastes run to the less refined and less stylishly elaborate. He could have lived in a tiny cottage in the woods nearby forever. He was a woodcutter by trade decades ago.

It is silly of me to be elaborating this to you. You are so vast in your capacities; you must see all of this already."

"I can and do but love hearing it from your mesmerizing lips. Tell me anything, everything that satisfies your needs and whims to express. I am here for you Viktoria."

"Very well then, Marius," she murmured with eyes alight in richness of him.

Viktoria continued in this manner, "Claire's parents, Henry and Adelaide, owned this manor. They are deceased and possession passed to Claire and her husband, which, of course, is Juria. They care for their children, Hansel and Gretel, excessively. Hansel and Gretel bound in and out of our abode here. They are young adults and cherish travel. They go everywhere with each other. Neither has ever married. Vampires rarely do."

The insouciance of her explanation did not escape Marius.

"Their own company seems to be all that they require. They are a lovely sight together.

Let's see now though. The layout, I have to describe the plateau's layout to you in full. The manor house is there, and then the church and cemetery are next in the ring. The church has almost tumbled from nonexistent use! Our distillery is next, stables on a line opposite the manor house as well. It is your and my guesthouse which promenades after the stables." The corners of her mouth lifted subtly as she uttered that.

Last are the no longer operated cook and staff quarters and the untended vineyards proximate.

As you recognize, this that we now stand on is the central garden. It is big, beautiful and lush. Claire manages it with a regularity and gusto that astounds me. Her blossoms are worth every instant that she spends on her knees in the soil in the dark though.

We have a steady water supply from an underground spring for the plants, flowers, our hygiene and washing our clothing. We are a fastidious little group. And, obviously, the drinking of the water is superfluous.

The base of the plateau where the Black Forest meets its lowest elevation is overgrown with wooded tangle. The road that once led here went unattended and has eroded into oblivion. And finally, when Henry and Adelaide's funeral was complete, staff of any kind were no longer required and released immediately.

We are a community unto ourselves now; forgotten and never visited. It is our perfect retreat and sanctuary."

Marius was well pleased.

Chapter 42

MORE TALE TO TELL

As vampires will, contrary to conventional notions, each was precipitate in their comfort with one another. The inked black night outside was calm; one of those sure calms that was not going to break into cracked sound or heaving wind. No raindrops had graced the dry earth here at length either. Indoors, food and drink not being required, the small group settled in and around the breakfast nook table.

Marius had his love, Viktoria, beside him. That gentled him more than all else. It satisfied him uniformly that Juria and Claire were as content with one another as he and Viktoria were.

Viktoria pressed Claire, "Marius perceives all in the past and present, much more so than we are capable. He understands that you have more tales to tell than where he ceased in his journal, his tome. He informed me of when he ended the writing of it; when he was ultimately able to leave my side. He girded up his emotional strength and sought out other lands, other avenues for his life; venues that would distract him from his recent past.

So he knows your tales but, as with me, he wishes your rendering of the facts. And it is quite a fascinating endeavor that we took to arrive here.

I long for your recollections too. The three of us have never really reminisced about this."

"Yes please, Claire and Juria, enlighten me as to your perspective. That is quite important to me. It serves to reign in my arrogance additionally as I find that I miss nuances within my psychic pictures unless I hear it from others. That humbles me as I learn my deficiencies. And I need that to maintain balance and best outlooks." Marius reassured himself, Juria and Claire with these comments.

Juria replied, "Thank you, Marius. Claire is the wordsmith between us. I will add to her interpretation when and if necessary."

Laughing then, he followed with, "So I will likely remain silent throughout!"

Claire stroked the back of Juria's neck and said, "Your eloquence, Juria, is level with mine. But I love you for saying otherwise."

Viktoria recommended, "Begin with your and Juria's difference of opinion of me when we returned to our respective cottages." Her eyes gleamed and she was excited to hear their version of events and whether she agreed with them or not.

"Much had transpired as we ultimately rescued Hansel and Gretel from a frightening foe. Juria and I grew close to Viktoria in that process until a night of sorrow came where Viktoria informed me of very ill news. Viktoria was distraught and I was heartbroken. I attempted to understand the complexities, and even though riddled with pain myself, I forgave Viktoria her inadvertent deed. She by then had bolted though. All I was privy to was that she abandoned her forested cottage.

Of course, I informed Juria of the harsh happenings upon his appearance after a day of diligent work." She glanced at Juria and smoothed her hand gently down his cheek. He smiled and flushed in the remembrance of it all.

"It was a rank moment as Juria reacted heavily. He lashed out at Viktoria's actions, ignored my appeals to his better judgment and set off to locate and destroy her. He felt she was ultimately evil and without an ounce of control."

Viktoria winced at that characterization of her.

"That was a crushing time for me. Juria was as if a madman and darted into the woods on what I figured was a trek of his to do you in, Viktoria.

But Viktoria could fly and has majestic powers. What were the odds of Juria's actually managing to do her harm unless finding her tomb in the light of day? He was irrational and unprepared besides. I had never observed him such prior and hope to never again.

He was not about to return to me or the children shortly. All I thought to do was bring Hansel and Gretel to my loving, doting parents and leave them in their care while I chased Juria in his vain pursuit of Viktoria.

And my love, your trail that I followed was effortlessly found. You were as if a charging elephant and you did not give a damn what traces you left in your wake."

"And you proceeded to catch me several days later, winded, hungry and without a true idea as to how to catch the one that I deemed villainous and without heart or soul."

"Hmmmm. I did do just that. I discovered you and, thankfully, your anger had been stretched and pounded into a more subdued piece of material by then. You were approachable on the subject, malleable almost.

I had planned in my journey from the manor where you had not planned at all. I, therefore, brought food and fed you on the spot. We vividly discussed our differences then. You resisted my logic over and over. And I would not be shamed into appealing to you sexually. I saw you weakening as time flowed. I was persuasive as I sincerely believed all that I poured out to you. It was never simple arm twisting. I was as if a zealot and you softened gradually under my storm of belief.

You see, I was sure of Viktoria's heart and soul as you were not."

Juria applied two fingers to his slightly puckered lips and then turned them to lie upon hers. He recognized that she had saved him from actions and hatred based upon misguided sentiment.

Who was he, after all, to judge others and declare his path the only one?

Chapter 43

HANSEL AND GRETEL

Dawn was measured carefully by those who were its slaughtered victims. Claire paced herself more rapidly as light of day crept toward them.

"Juria allowed me to take him back to our humble abode where he and I briefly recovered for twenty four hours. We concluded that Viktoria was no longer our business."

Viktoria interrupted to add, "My vision failed me throughout this period. My emotions flailed away at my ability to function and I was absolutely useless to myself. I was incoherent and lucky that I found hapless animals to quench my need. As to secure shelter during the day, I had only a single place in mind. I did not even fly there; I staggered there."

Claire agreed. "Her plight was horrendous as we discovered later.

But, as I was mentioning before, when Juria and I had regained our stamina, we set out to visit my parents in order to collect the children. It was a reunion that we hugely anticipated and we readied ourselves for the sight of delightful faces, young and old.

It was as we hoped. We were welcomed by all. Hansel and Gretel set upon us in their happiness at having their father and stepmother safely back . . . . and together.

Night's ledge expanded until no exterior light remained on our first day there."

Claire gazed at Viktoria then.

"We were shocked as Viktoria limply shuffled into the dining area where we were gathered to eat dinner. The staff had served us and already retired to their quarters.

You definitely frightened Juria and me. Strangely, to the two of us, my parents, Hansel and Gretel were calm and motionless. Juria clenched his fists upon first sight of you. How absurd, though, as if fists were remotely a match against you. I quietly clutched those fists of his and they relaxed and anger vanished into fingers without tension."

Viktoria swept in. "My strength was renewed some as Henry and Adelaide never forsook me. They gave me shelter as soon as I collapsed onto their doorstep. I moaned for their mercy and aid. I was yet capable of taking their blood then and there but I would not do that! They cherished my earlier bravery. So they released the guest house to me and said that 'it is yours.' I went to the lower floor there and managed to stumble into that wood shell, closed the lid and slowly begin retrieving my faculties.

Juria took over then briefly. "You were nowhere near a complete revival when you came upon Claire and me. I am so glad that Claire's touch returned me to my senses."

Then Claire interjected. "And you, wonderful Viktoria, offered us an opportunity that Juria and I yielded to. We loved your being then and sought to be the same; me the most, Juria less so. The two of us proffered our necks and trusted you as never before."

Viktoria breathlessly exclaimed, "I seized upon that as I was absolutely aware of the formula for turning one. All I had to do was care for you and lance your neck as well. My feeding was lustily done but was secondary to my creating everlasting life for you both!"

You were sated but asked my parents if they chose to partake of eternal existence. They were satisfied with their human manifestation and refused your offer. They lived barely longer and then passed within days of one another.

I will always feel blessed that I was their daughter!

We all agreed that Hansel and Gretel were to be turned only at their request and only once past adolescence when they could really decide competently."

Marius stated, "In your words, convey to me what their selection was."

"They were enamored of what they observed as Viktoria, Juria and I associated beautifully together. We also provided their sustenance as long as they required food and drink.

They agonized into and through their teens regarding the nightly bloodlettings which were primal nature for us.

Ultimately, they decided that the extended benefits they planned on providing the world outweighed the carnage that they would require to maintain themselves. And so, they too, allowed Viktoria to bestow the undead reward upon them when in their middle twenties.

They have yet to perform beneficially. They prize travel and dabble in mischief. Someday they will remember their reason behind their change.

They are glorious to look at. Hansel is tall and brawny, chiseled of face. Gretel is petal soft in appearance, devastatingly appealing in visage and shape."

Marius understood that Hansel and Gretel had peered into Viktoria's essence as they had been insistently curious. He also recognized that Viktoria permitted it as she had no secrets that she was afraid of; therefore, she let them learn through her experience.

Her great passion for Marius piqued Hansel and Gretel's inquisitiveness the greatest. And, they considered, if he could love Viktoria so intensely, how was he able to love Amanda in addition? This was a conundrum.

They became determined to meet this woman and be brought to a heightened sense of the mechanics of love. Hansel and Gretel were new and unpracticed in their vampire's visionary abilities. They penetrated Amanda's thought processes wherever she was and wherever they were. Her emotions remained murky yet to Hansel and Gretel; observation they decided had to come directly.

Hansel and Gretel, Marius comprehended, were in Seattle.

Chapter 44

RIPPED ASUNDER

They strolled from the manor house to what was now their guesthouse.

"I must apologize to you my lovely Viktoria. I seem to have regressed miserably since re-experiencing the paradise that is your love for me. The feeling is akin to that of the shiest of teenager overwhelmed at daring to approach the perceived out of reach object of his surging sentiment. He becomes swallowed by what otherwise might be considered mundane but instead carves into him a permanent message of signatory instants; your clasp of my hand, our fingers meshed and attuned, the quick delicious tang of your smile, the tiny filaments of your fragile hair at neck nape shining in moonlight which then gives off a brief gossamer glow.

You overwhelm me tonight my lustrous queen. Forgive me my rare timid and awestruck attitude with you. My happiness leaves me at your behest.

Lead me where you will. I cannot resist you any longer. Show me your desires and I will become exclusively that instrument that fits your every need."

And Viktoria brought him into the spacious upper floor of their special quarters.

Sun's dazzle was an hour away or some more.

Viktoria quaked at her dominance over Marius. She recognized it as being short lived. And she had a passion for him that did not include control; she lusted for that with all others but not him. Her fundaments required only overall equivalence between them. Let the fragments of imbalance ebb and flow. It mattered not as their regard for the other was, like the sea, to wash over the irregularities and form it into a beach's sandy smooth character.

At her direction, Marius sat. She removed his heavy boots first and was not able to resist dragging her long fingernails over his bulging jeans material and thereby released his swollen form. She did not otherwise touch him.

He was supremely hard for her already but waited upon her slow, sensual maneuvers. His anticipation filled his cock intensively and it was very difficult for him not to touch himself or her. Yet he kept his promise of permitting her lead in this coupling.

She commanded that he remain passive.

Her delicate raiment's hid nothing from his hungry eyes. He placed his flat palms on his thighs, his itch for stimulation saturating his being. He stared at her and then stared at his looming, greatly risen column of cock that towered before them both. He silently begged for tactile attention from her. She ignored his invisible plea entirely.

She challenged his passion's patience throughout. It aroused her critically to play upon him and observe his heat quicken into fire. She played upon him in many ways. She disrobed fully before him, swaying sensuously as she did so. She teased him and loved it as she fondled her own very ample bosom. She created a nearly streaming wetness within herself by grasping her long black nipples; twisting them for a second or two and then pulling them toward him. Her nipples firmed under these ministrations and she moaned feverishly.

She finally approached him. From his rent material, she inspected his excitement protruding. He was groaning for richer contact from her then.

She gave it to him because she was now beyond restraint herself. She kneeled to a single knee, wrapped both hands around his swollen shaft and pummeled his extremely rounded and broadened cockhead with lashing tongue, sealed sucking lips and pumping hands.

And then she stopped. She drew down to both knees and avoided his reddened, pulsing monstrosity between his legs. She insured he was not able to relieve himself when she clamped her hands down upon his wrists and chair arms. He was helpless in any use of his upper extremities.

She sucked his nipples, left then right. His cock jerked frequently all on its own from the intense pleasure that Viktoria was providing his chest.

Simultaneously, Claire and Juria had retreated to their section of the manor house. Claire was in vast and delightful submission to Juria as they wove their sexual cloth; cloth which was about to ignite into intense blues, yellows and reds.

Juria thrust into Claire in a hard, slashing rhythm. She was supine with her legs angled up to and extended over his taut shoulders. He leaned into her legs as he leaned into her torso; he enabled himself to tend to her hot nipples with his mouth, inadvertently spread her legs further apart and drove deeper into her with every subsequent stroke. She gasped as he did this. Juria also held her wrists down upon the covered flooring as he stretched them above her head. Her eyes were squeezed shut as she panted for breath between her escalating moans.

Viktoria took mercy upon Marius at long last. She faced away from him, spread her wet nether lips apart and backed onto his crimson tool in a squat. She begged for him to remain still as she slid him fully into her; whereupon she pounded his raging cock up and down, over and over.

Juria rode his vampire wife in ever accelerating motion. As he lodged himself delightfully into her, he recognized that her threshold had almost been breached. Her vault and inner thighs started to tremble. This tremble goaded him on.

Viktoria moved in a blur. Precipitously, she ground Marius's length into her completely, froze and then cried out. Her spasms racked Marius and he surrendered to her appetite. His jets boomed against her interior and his cock expanded even more in the throes of their mutual ecstasy.

Claire's trembles surged into molten waves and primed Juria for his tearing release. Mutual gratification was delivered and seemed limitless; was profound.

The four vampires were ripped asunder in their huge adoration for their partners.

That they were sated in a common second portended nothing except that eros was capable of blessing the entire world if allowed to.

Her lid was scaled. Marius was in process of doing similarly. Claire and Juria followed suit.

A notion shot through his synapses just prior to sinking into undead paralysis. He had not yet divulged to Viktoria his true age ever. He was nearly as ancient as Adam and Eve's raging offspring; he was Cain's firstborn son, Mezopx. Septimius Severus and Cinaed MacAlpin owed their lives to him as well. He had not been Marius always. Definitely not!

Marius was merely his noblest self.

And Viktoria was possibly his greatest love.

About The Author

Jeffrey Underwood graduated from the University of Washington with a degree in psychology. Though he has practiced as a Registered Nurse for many years, he comes from a family of published authors. This is his second foray into the realm of erotic fantasy. His first published work was the Forbidden Tome; Hansel and Gretel's True Tale. He currently resides in Mountlake Terrace, Washington, a suburb of Seattle, and again hopes that those who read this second offering of his enjoy the time spent.